"There Hasn't Been A Man. Not One."

Meg stared up at Steven fearlessly, her eyes wide and quiet. "There isn't time in my life for that sort of emotional turmoil. I've worked too hard, too long, to go looking for complications."

She started to turn away, but his lean, strong hands were on her waist, stilling her, exciting her.

"Your honesty is going to land you in hot water one day."

"Why lie?" she asked.

"Why, indeed?" he replied huskily.

Steven drew her closer, resting his chin on the top of her blond head, and her heart raced wildly as his fingers slid slowly up and down from her waist to her rib cage.

"What if I give in to that last bit of provocation?" he whispered roughly.

"What provocation?"

His teeth closed softly on her earlobe, his warm breath brushing her cheek. "Your bed or mine, Meg?"

Dear Reader,

Welcome to August! As I promised last month, August's *Man of the Month* title is by one of your favorites—and mine—Diana Palmer. It's called *Night of Love,* and this story really is something wonderful and special.

The rest of August is equally terrific. First, there's *Kane's Way* by Dixie Browning. You know, it's hard to believe that this talented lady has written over *fifty* books for Silhouette! And they all just keep getting better and better.

Next comes a fun-filled story from Lass Small. The title of Lass's latest is *Balanced,* but I'm not sure that our hero and heroine feel exactly "balanced" for most of the book... more like *off*-balanced from love.

The month is completed by delightful, sensuous, sparkling stories from Cathie Linz, Linda Turner and Barbara McCauley. And as for September, well, have we got some great stuff in store for you. Look for new series by Ann Major *and* Joan Hohl, as well as some delightful tales from four other fabulous writers.

So, until next month, happy reading.

Lucia Macro
Senior Editor

DIANA PALMER
NIGHT OF LOVE

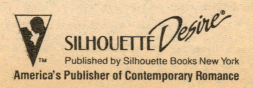

SILHOUETTE *Desire*®
Published by Silhouette Books New York
America's Publisher of Contemporary Romance

SILHOUETTE BOOKS
300 East 42nd St., New York, N.Y. 10017

NIGHT OF LOVE

Copyright © 1993 by Diana Palmer

ISBN: 0-373-05799-7

First Silhouette Books printing August 1993

All the characters in this book have no existence outside the
imagination of the author and have no relation whatsoever to
anyone bearing the same name or names. They are not even
distantly inspired by any individual known or unknown to the
author, and all incidents are pure invention.

Books by Diana Palmer

Silhouette Desire

Silhouette Special Edition

Silhouette Romance

Silhouette Books

Also by Diana Palmer

*Long, Tall Texans
‡Most Wanted Series

For Judy

Prologue

Steven Ryker paced his office at Ryker Air with characteristic energy, smoking a cigarette that he hated while he turned the air blue in quiet muttering. A chapter of his life that he'd closed the door on four years past had reopened, leaving his emotional wounds bare and bleeding.

Meg was back.

He didn't recognize his own fear. It wasn't a condition he'd ever associated with himself. But things had changed. He'd gone through a period of mourning when Meg had walked out on him to begin a balletic career in New York. He'd consoled himself with woman after willing woman. But in the end, he'd been alone with the painful memories. They hurt, and because they still hurt, he blamed Meg. He wanted her to suffer as he had. He wanted to see her beautiful blue eyes fill with tears, he wanted to see pain on that exquisite face framed by soft blond hair. He wanted consolation for the hell she'd put him through by leaving without a word when she'd promised to be his wife.

He put out the cigarette. It was a habit, like loving Meg. He hated both: cigarettes and the blond memory from his past. He'd never had a woman jilt him. Of course, he'd never asked a woman to marry him, either. He'd been content to live alone, until Meg had kissed him in gratitude for the present he'd given her when she turned eighteen. His life had turned over then.

Their fathers, hers and his, had become business partners when Meg was fourteen and her brother, David, just a little older. The families had developed a closeness that tied their lives together. Meg had been a sweet nuisance that Steven had tolerated when he and David had become best friends. But the nuisance grew up into a beautiful, regal woman who'd melted the ice around his hard heart. He'd given everything he was, everything he had, to Meg. And it hadn't been enough.

He couldn't forgive her for not wanting him. He couldn't admit that his obsession with her had all but cost him his sanity when she left. He wanted vengeance. He wanted Meg.

There would be a way to make her pay, he vowed. She'd hurt her leg and couldn't dance temporarily. But that ballet company she worked for was in real financial straits. If he played his cards right, he might yet have that one magical night in Meg's arms that he'd dreamed of for years. But this time, it wouldn't be out of love and need. It would be out of vengeance. Meg was back. And he was going to make her pay for what she'd made of him.

One

Meg was already out of humor when she went to answer the phone. She'd been in the middle of her exercises at the bar, and she hated interruptions that diverted her concentration. An injury had forced her into this temporary hiatus at her family home in Wichita, Kansas. It was hard enough to do the exercises in the first place with a damaged ligament in her ankle. It didn't help her mood when she picked up the receiver and found one of Steven Ryker's women on the other end of the line.

Steven, the president of Ryker Air, had been playing tennis all afternoon with Meg's brother, David. He'd obviously forwarded his calls here. It irritated Meg to have to talk to his women friends at all. But then, she'd always been possessive about Steven Ryker; long before she left Wichita for New York to study ballet.

"Is Steve there?" a feminine voice demanded.

Another in a long line of Steve's corporate lovers, no doubt, Meg thought angrily. Well, this one was going to become a lost cause. Right now.

"Who's calling, please?" Meg drawled.

There was a pause. "This is Jane. Who are you?"

"I'm Meg," she replied pertly, trying not to laugh.

"Oh." The voice hesitated. "Well, I'd like to speak to Steve, please."

Meg twirled the cord around her finger and lowered her voice an octave. "Darling?" she purred, her lips close to the receiver. "Oh, darling, do wake up. It's Jane, and she wants to speak to you."

There was a harsh intake of breath on the other end of the line. Meg stifled a giggle, because she could almost read the woman's mind. Her blue eyes twinkled in her soft oval face, framed by pale blond hair drawn into a disheveled bun atop her head.

"I have *never...!*" An outraged voice exploded in her ear.

"Oh, you really should, you know," Meg interrupted, sighing theatrically. "He's so *marvelous* in bed! Steven, darling...?"

The phone was slammed in her ear loud enough to break an eardrum. Meg put a slender hand over her mouth as she replaced the receiver in its cradle. Take that, Steven, she thought.

She turned and walked gingerly back into the room David had converted from the old ballroom into a practice room for his sister. It didn't get a lot of use, since she was in New York most of the year now, but it was a wonderfully thoughtful extravagance on her brother's part. David, like Meg, had shares in Ryker Air. David was a vice president of the company as well. But the old family fortune had been sacrificed by their late father in an attempt to take over the company, just before his death. He'd lost, and the company had very nearly folded. Except for the uncanny business acumen of Steven Ryker, it would have. Steve pulled the irons out of the fire and made the company solvent. He owned most of it now. And he should, Meg thought charitably. Heaven knew, he'd worked hard enough for it all these years.

As she exercised, Meg felt wicked. She shouldn't have caused Steve problems with his current love. They hadn't been engaged for four years, and she'd long ago relinquished the right to feel possessive about him.

Pensively she picked up her towel and wrapped it around her long, graceful neck, over the pink leotard she wore with her leg warmers and her pitiful-looking toe shoes. She stared down at them ruefully. They were so expensive that she had to wear her old ones for practice, and anyone seeing her in them would be convinced that she was penniless. That was almost the truth. Because despite the shares of stock she held in Ryker Air—the company that Steven's father and Meg and David's father had founded jointly—Meg *was* practically destitute. She was only a minor dancer in the New York ballet company she'd joined just a year ago, after three years of study with a former prima ballerina who had a studio in New York. She had yet to perform her first solo role. Presumably when she passed that landmark, she'd be higher paid, more in demand. Unless she missed a jump, that was, as she had a week ago. The memory was painful, like her ankle. That sort of clumsiness wasn't going to get her any starring roles. And now she had the added worry of getting her damaged tendon back in shape. The exercise, recommended and outlined by a physical therapist, was helping. But it was torturously slow, and very painful, to exercise those muscles. It had to be done carefully, too, so that she wouldn't damage them even further.

She went back into her disciplined exercises with a determined smile still on her face. She tried to concentrate on fluidity of movement and not the inevitable confrontation when Steve found out what she'd said to his girlfriend. Her whole life seemed to have been colored by him, since she was fourteen and their fathers had become business partners. Her father had worshiped Steven from the beginning. So had David. But Meg had hated him on sight.

For the first few years, she'd fought him tooth and nail, not bothering to hide her animosity. But on the eve of her eighteenth birthday, things had changed between them quite suddenly. He'd given her a delicate pearl necklace and she'd kissed him for it, a little shyly. Except that she'd missed his lean cheek and found his hard, rough mouth instead.

In all fairness, he'd been every bit as shocked as Meg. But instead of pulling away and making a joke of it, there had quite suddenly been a second kiss; one that couldn't be mistaken for anything but a passionate, almost desperate exchange. When it ended, neither of them had spoken. Steven's silver eyes had flashed dangerously and he'd left the room abruptly, without saying a single word.

But that kiss had changed the way they looked at each other. Their relationship had changed, too. Reluctantly, almost helplessly, Steven had started taking her out on dates and within a month, he proposed marriage. She'd wanted ballet so much by that time that despite her raging desire and love for Steve, she was torn between marriage and dancing. Steven, apparently sensing that, had turned up the heat. A long bout of lovemaking had almost ended in intimacy. Steven had lost control and his unbounded ardor had frightened Meg. An argument had ensued, and he'd said some cruel things to her.

That same evening, after their argument, Steven had taken his former mistress, Daphne, out on the town very publicly, and an incriminating photo of the couple had appeared in the society column of the daily newspaper the next day.

Meg had been devastated. She'd cried herself to sleep. Rather than face Steven and fight for a relationship with him, she'd opted to leave and go to New York to study ballet.

Like a coward, Meg had run. But what she'd seen spoke for itself and her heart was broken. If Steven could go to another woman that quickly, he certainly wasn't the type to stay faithful after he was married. Steven had been so ardent that it was miraculous she was still a virgin, anyway.

All of those facts raised doubts, the biggest one being that Steven had probably only wanted to marry her to keep all the stock from the partnership in the family. It had seemed quite logical at the time. Everyone knew how ambitious Steven was, and he and his father hadn't been too happy at some of the changes Meg's father had wanted to make at the time of the engagement.

Meg had gone to New York on the first plane out of Wichita, to be met by one of her mother's friends and set up in a small apartment near the retired prima ballerina with whom she would begin her studies.

Nicole, meanwhile, met Steve for coffee and explained that Meg had left town. Afterward, Meg heard later, Steven had gotten roaring drunk for the first, last and only time in his life. An odd reaction for a man who only wanted to marry her for her shares of stock, and who'd thrown her out of his life. But Steven hadn't called or written, and he never alluded to the brief time they'd spent as a couple. His behavior these days was as cold as he'd become himself.

Steve hadn't touched her since their engagement. But his eyes had, in a way that made her knees weak. It was a good thing that she spent most of her time in New York. Otherwise, if she'd been around Steven very much, she might have fallen headlong into an affair with him. She wouldn't have been able to resist him, and he was experienced enough to know that. He'd made sure that she kept her distance and he kept his. But the lingering passion she felt for him hadn't dimmed over the years. It was simply buried, so that it wouldn't interfere with her dreams of becoming a prima ballerina. She'd forced herself to settle; she'd chosen not to fight for his love. Her life since had hardly been a happy one, but she told herself that she was content.

Steve still came to the Shannon house to see David, and the families got together at the annual company picnics and benefits. These days, the family meant Steven and his mother and Meg and her brother David, because the older Shannons were dead now.

Mason Ryker, Steven's father, and John and Nicole Shannon had died in the years since Meg went to New York; Mason of a heart attack, and John and Nicole in a private plane crash the very year Meg had left Wichita. Amy Ryker was as protective of Meg as if she'd been her mother instead of Steve's, but she lived in West Palm Beach now and only came home when she had to. She and Steven had never really been able to bear each others' company.

Steven had women hanging from the chandeliers, from what Amy told Meg on the occasions when she came to New York to watch Meg dance. He was serious about none of them, and there had never been a whisper of a serious commitment since his brief engagement to Meg.

Meg herself had become buried in her work. All she lived and breathed was the dance. The hours every day of grueling practice, the dieting and rigid life-style she lived made relationships difficult if not impossible. She often thought she was a little cold as a woman. Since Steven, she'd never felt her innocence threatened. Men had dated her, of course, but she was too conscious of the dangers to risk the easy life-styles some of the older dancers had once indulged in. These days, a one-night stand could be life-threatening. Besides, Meg thought sadly, only Steven had ever made her want intimacy. Her memories of him were devastating sometimes, despite the violent passion he'd shown her the last time they'd been together.

She stretched her aching muscles, and her mind wandered back to the mysterious Jane who'd telephoned. Who the hell was Jane? she wondered, and what did Steven want with someone who could speak that haughtily over the phone? She pictured a milky little blonde with a voluptuous figure and stretched even harder.

It was time to take off the lean roast and cottage potatoes she was cooking for supper by the time David walked in the door, still in his tennis outfit, looking as pleasant and jovial as ever. He had the same coloring his sister had, but he was shorter and a little broader than she.

He grinned at her. "Just thought I might mention that you're in it up to your neck. Steve got a call while we were at his house, and your goose is about to be cooked."

She stopped dead in the hall as Steven Ryker walked in behind her brother. Steve was a little over six feet tall, very dark and intimidating. He reminded her of actors who played mobsters, because he had the same threatening look about him, and even a deep scar down one cheek. It had probably been put there by some jealous woman in his checkered past, she thought venomously, but it gave him a rakish look.

Even his eyes were unusual. They were a cross between ice blue and watered gray, and they could almost cut the skin when they looked as they did at the moment. The white shorts he was wearing left the muscular length of his tanned, powerful legs bare. A white knit shirt did the same for his arms. He was incredibly fit for a man on the wrong side of thirty-five who sat at a desk all day.

Right now he looked very casual, dressed in his tennis outfit, and that was the most deceptive thing about him. He was never casual. He always played to win, even at sports. He was also the most sensuous, sexy man she'd ever known. Or ever would. Just looking at him made her weak-kneed. She hid her reaction to him as she always had, in humor.

"Ah, Steven." Meg sighed, batting her long eyelashes at him. "How lovely to see you. Did one of your women die, or is there some simpler reason that we're being honored by your presence?"

"Pardon me while I go out back and skin a rock," David mumbled with a grin, diving quickly past his sister in a most ungentlemanly way to get out of the line of fire.

"Coward!" she yelled after him as the door slammed.

"You wouldn't need protection if you could learn to keep your mouth shut, Mary Margaret," Steven said with a cool smile. "I'd had my calls forwarded here while I was playing tennis. Jane couldn't believe what she'd heard, so she telephoned my home again and got me. It so happened David and I had stopped back by the house to look at a new painting I'd bought. I canceled the call forwarding just in time—or I might have been left in blissful ignorance."

She glared at him. "It was your own fault. You don't have to have your women telephone you here!"

The glitter in his eyes got worse. "Jealous, Meg?" he taunted.

"Of you? God forbid," she said as casually as she could, and with a forced smile. "Of course I do remember vividly the wonderful things you can do with your hands and those hard lips, darling, but I'm quite urbane these days and less easily impressed."

"Careful," he warned softly. "You may be more vulnerable than you realize."

She backed down. "Anyway," she muttered, "why don't you just take Jane Thingamabob out for a steak and warm her back up again?"

"Jane Dray is my mother's maiden aunt," he said after a minute, watching her reaction with amusement. "You might remember her from the last company picnic?"

Meg did, with horror. The old dowager was a people-eater of the first order, who probably still wore corsets and cursed modern transportation. "Oh, dear," she began.

"She is now horrified that her favorite great-nephew is sleeping with little Meggie Shannon, who used to be such a sweet, innocent child."

"Oh, my God," Meg groaned, leaning against the wall.

"Yes. And she'll more than likely rush to tell *your* great-aunt Henrietta, who will feel obliged to write to my mother in West Palm Beach and tell her the scandalous news that you are now a scarlet woman. And my mother, who always has preferred you to me, will naturally assume that I seduced you, not the reverse.''

"Damn!" she moaned. "This is all your fault!"

He folded his arms over his broad chest. "You brought it on yourself. Don't blame me. I'm sure my mother will be utterly shocked at your behavior, nevertheless, especially since she's taken great pains to try to make up for the loss of your own mother years ago."

"I'll kill myself!" she said dramatically.

"Could you fix supper first?" David asked, sticking his head around the kitchen door. "I'm starved. So is Steve."

"Then why don't the two of you go out to a restaurant?" she asked, still reeling from her horrid mistake.

"Heartless woman." David sighed. "And I was so looking forward to the potatoes and roast I can smell cooking on the stove."

He managed to look pitiful and thin, all at the same time. She glared at him. "Well, I suppose I can manage supper. As if you need feeding up! Look at you!"

"I'm a walking monument of your culinary skills," David argued. "If I could cook, I'd look healthy between your vacations."

"It isn't exactly a vacation," Meg murmured worriedly. "The ballet company I work for is between engagements, and when there's no money to pay the light bill, we can't keep the theater open. Our manager is looking for more financing even now."

"He'll find it," David consoled her. "It's an established ballet company, and he's a good finance man. Stop brooding."

"Okay," she said.

"Do we have time to shower and change?" David asked.

"Sure," she told him. "I need to do that myself. I've been working out all afternoon."

"You push yourself too hard," Steve remarked coolly. "Is it really worth it?"

"Of course!" she said. She smiled outrageously. "Don't you know that ballerinas are the ideal ornament for rich gentlemen?" she added, lying through her teeth. "I actually had a patron offer to keep me." She didn't add that the man had adoption, not seduction, in mind, and that he was the caretaker at her apartment house.

Incredibly Steve's eyes began to glitter. "What did you tell him?"

"That I pay my own way, of course." She laughed. She held on to the railing of the long staircase and leaned forward. "Tell you what, Steve. If you play your cards right, when I get to the top of the ladder and start earning what I'm really worth, I'll keep you."

He tried not to smile, but telltale lines rippled around his firm, sculptured mouth.

"You're impossible." David chuckled.

"I make your taciturn friend smile, though," she added, watching Steve with twinkling eyes. "I don't think he knew how until I came along. I keep his temper honed, too."

"Be careful that I don't hone it on you," he cautioned quietly. There was something smoldering in his eyes, something tightly leashed. There always had been, but when he was around her, just lately, it threatened to escape.

She laughed, because the look in those gunmetal-gray eyes made her nervous. "I won't provoke you, Steven," she said. "I'm not quite that brave." He scowled and she changed the subject. "I'm sorry about Aunt Jane," she added with sincere apology. "I'll call her and explain, if you like."

"There's no need," he said absently, his gaze intent on her flushed face. "I've already taken care of it."

As usual. She could have said it, but she didn't. Steven didn't let grass grow under his feet. He was an accomplished mover and shaker, which was why his company was still solvent when others had gone bankrupt. She made a slight movement with her shoulders and proceeded up the staircase. She felt his eyes on her, but she didn't look back.

When Meg had showered and changed into a lacy white pantsuit, she went back downstairs. She'd left her long blond hair in a knot, because she knew how much Steven disliked it up. Her blue eyes twinkled with mischief.

Steve had changed, too, and returned from his house, which was barely two blocks away. He was wearing white slacks with a soft blue knit shirt, and he looked elegant and unapproachable. His back was broad, his shoulders straining against the expensive material of his shirt. Meg remembered without wanting to how it had felt all those years ago to run her hands up and down that expanse of muscle while he kissed her. There was a thick pelt of hair over his chest and stomach. During their brief interlude, she'd learned the hard contours of his body with delight. He could have had her anytime during that one exquisite month of togetherness, but he'd always drawn back in time. She wondered sometimes if he'd ever regretted it. Secretly she did. There would never be anyone else that she'd want as she had wanted Steve. The memories would have been bittersweet if they'd been lovers, but at least they might fill the emptiness she felt now. Her life was dedicated to ballet and as lonely as death. No man touched her, except her ballet partners, and none of them excited her.

She'd always been excited by Steven. That hadn't faded. The past two times she'd come home to visit David, the hunger she felt for her ex-fiancé had grown unexpectedly, until it actually frightened her. *He* frightened her, with his vast experience of women and his intent way of looking at her.

He turned when he heard her enter the room, with a cigarette in his hand. He quit smoking periodically, sometimes with more success than others. He was restless and high-strung, and the cigarette seemed to calm him. Fortunately, the house was air-conditioned and David had, at Meg's insistence, added a huge filtering system to it. There was no smell of smoke.

"Nasty habit," she muttered, glaring at him.

He inclined his head toward her with a mocking smile. "Doesn't your great-aunt Henrietta dip snuff...?"

She sighed. "Yes, she does. You look very much as your father used to," she murmured.

He shook his head. "He was shorter."

"But just as somber. You don't smile, Steve," she said quietly, and moved gracefully into the big front room with its modern black and white and chrome furniture and soft honey-colored carpet.

"Smiling doesn't fit my image," he returned.

"Some image," she mused. "I saw one of your vice presidents hide in a hangar when he spotted you on the tarmac. That lazy walk of yours lets everyone know when you're about to lose your temper. So slow and easy—so deadly."

"It gets results," he replied, indicating that he was aware of the stance and probably used it to advantage with his people. "Have you seen a balance sheet lately? Aren't you interested in what I'm doing with your stock?"

"Finance doesn't mean much to me," she confessed. "I'm much more interested in the ballet company I'm working with. It really is in trouble."

"Join another company," he said.

"I've spent a year working my way up in this one," she returned. "I can't start all over again. Ballerinas don't have that long, as a rule. I'm going on twenty-three."

"So old?" His eyes held hers. "You look very much as you did at eighteen. More sophisticated, of course. The girl I used to know would have died before she'd have insinuated to a perfect stranger that she was sharing my bed."

"I thought she was one of your women," Meg muttered. "God knows, you've got enough of them. I'll bet you have to keep a computer file so you won't forget their names. No wonder Jane believed I was one of them without question!"

"You could have been, once," he reminded her bluntly. "But I got noble and pushed you away in the nick of time." He laughed without humor. "I thought we'd have plenty of time for intimate discoveries after we were married. More fool me." He lifted the cigarette to his mouth, and his eyes were ice-cold.

"I was grass green back then," she reminded him with what she hoped was a sophisticated smile. "You'd have been disappointed."

He blew out a soft cloud of smoke and his eyes searched hers. "No. But you probably would have been. I wanted you too badly that last night we were together. I'd have hurt you."

It was the night they'd argued. But before that, they'd lain on his black leather sofa and made love until she'd begged him to finish it. She hadn't been afraid, then. But he hadn't. Even now, the sensations he'd kindled in her body made her flush.

"I don't think you would have, really," she said absently, her body tingling with forbidden memories as she looked at him. "Even so, I wanted you enough that I wouldn't have cared if you hurt me. I was wild to have you. I forgot all my fears."

He didn't notice the implication. He averted his eyes. "Not wild enough to marry me, of course."

"I was eighteen. You were thirty and you had a mistress."

His back stiffened. He turned, his eyes narrow, scowling. "What?"

"You know all this," she said uncomfortably. "My mother explained it to you the morning I left."

He moved closer, his lean face hard, unreadable. "Explain it to me yourself."

"Your father told me about Daphne," she faltered. "The night we argued, she was the one you took out, the one you were photographed with. Your father told me that you were only marrying me for the stock. He and your mother cared about me—perhaps more than my own did. When he said that you always went back to Daphne, no matter what, I got cold feet."

His high cheekbones flushed. He looked...stunned. "He told you that?" he asked harshly.

"Yes. Well, my mother knew about Daphne, too," she said heavily.

"Oh, God." He turned away. He leaned over to crush out his cigarette, his eyes bleak, hopeless.

"I knew you weren't celibate, but finding that you had a mistress was something of a shock, especially when we'd been seeing each other for a month."

"Yes. I expect it was a shock." He was staring down into the ashtray, unmoving. "I knew your mother was against the engagement. She had her heart set on helping you become a ballerina. She'd failed at it, but she was determined to see that you succeeded."

"She loved me..."

He turned, his dark eyes riveting to hers. "You ran, damn you."

She took a steadying breath. "I was eighteen. I had reasons for running that you don't know about." She dropped her eyes to his broad chest. "But I think I understand the way you were with me. You had Daphne. No wonder it was so easy for you to draw back when we made love."

His eyes closed. He almost shuddered with reaction. He shook with the force of his rage at his father and Meg's mother.

"It's all water under the bridge now, though," she said then, studying his rigid posture with faint surprise. "Steve?"

He took a long, deep breath and lit another cigarette. "Why didn't you say something? Why didn't you wait and talk to me?"

"There was no point," she said simply. "You'd already told me to get out of your life," she added with painful satisfaction.

"At the time, I probably meant it," he replied heavily. "But that didn't last long. Two days later, I was more then willing to start over, to try again. I came to tell you so. But you were gone."

"Yes." She stared at her slender hands, ringless, while her mind fought down the flood of misery she'd felt when she left Wichita. The fear had finally defeated her. And he didn't know . . .

"If you'd waited, I could have explained," he said tautly.

She looked at him sadly. "Steve, what could you have said? It was perfectly obvious that you weren't

ready to make a real commitment to me, even if you
were willing to marry me for your own reasons. And I
had some terrors that I couldn't face."

"Did you?" he asked dully. He lifted the cigarette
to his chiseled mouth and stared into space. "Your
father and mine were involved in a subtle proxy fight
about that time, did anyone tell you?"

"No. Why would they have needed to?"

"No reason," he said bitterly. "None at all."

She hated the way he looked. Surely what had happened in the past didn't still bother him. His pride had
suffered, though, that might explain it.

She moved closer, smiling gently. "Steve, it was
forever ago," she said. "We're different people now,
and all I did really was to spare us both a little embarrassment when we broke up. If you'd wanted me that
badly, you'd have come after me."

He winced. His dark silver eyes caught hers and
searched them with anguish. "You're sure of that."

"Of course. It was no big thing," she said softly.
"You've had dozens of women since, and your mother
says you don't take any of them any more seriously
than you took me. You enjoy being a bachelor. If I
wasn't ready for marriage, neither were you."

His face tautened. He smiled, but it was no smile at
all. "You're right," he said coldly, "it was no big
thing. One or two nights together would have cured
both of us. You were a novelty, you with your innocent body and big eyes. I wanted you, all right."

She searched his face, looking for any trace of soft-
ening. She didn't find it. She hated seeing him that
way, so somber and remote. Impishly she wiggled her

eyebrows. "Do you still? Feel like experimenting? Your bed or mine?"

He didn't smile. His eyes flashed, and one of them narrowed a little. That meant trouble.

He lifted the cigarette to his lips one more time, drawing out the silence until she felt like an idiot for what she'd suggested. He bent his tall frame to put it out in the ashtray, and she watched. He had beautiful hands: dark and graceful and long-fingered. On a woman's body, they were tender magic...

"No, thanks," he said finally. "I don't like being one in a queue."

Her eyebrows arched. "I beg your pardon?"

He straightened and stuck his hands deep into his pockets, emphasizing the powerful muscles in his thighs, his narrow hips and flat stomach. "Shouldn't you be looking after your roast? Or do you imagine that David and I don't have enough charcoal in our diets already?"

She moved toward him gracefully. "Steve, I dislike very much what you've just insinuated." She stared up at him fearlessly, her eyes wide and quiet. "There hasn't been a man. Not one. There isn't time in my life for the sort of emotional turmoil that comes from involvement. Emotional upsets influence the way I dance. I've worked too hard, too long, to go looking for complications."

She started to turn away, but his lean, strong hands were on her waist, stilling her, exciting her.

"Your honesty, Mary Margaret, is going to land you in hot water one day."

"Why lie?" she asked, peering over her shoulder at him.

"Why, indeed?" he asked huskily.

He drew her closer, resting his chin on the top of her blond head, and her heart raced wildly as his fingers slid slowly up and down from her waist to her rib cage.

"What if I give in to that last bit of provocation?" he whispered roughly.

"What provocation?"

His teeth closed softly on her earlobe, his warm breath brushing her cheek. "Your bed or mine, Meg?" he whispered.

Two

Meg wondered if she was still breathing. She'd been joking, but Steve didn't look or sound as if he were.

"Steve..." she whispered.

His eyes fell to her mouth as her head lay back against his broad chest. His face changed at the sound of his name on her lips. His hands on her waist contracted until they bruised and his face went rigid. "Mouth like a pink rose petal," he said in an oddly rough tone. "I almost took you once, Meg."

She felt herself vibrating, like drawn cord. "You pushed me away," she whispered.

"I had to!" There was anger in the silvery depths of his eyes. "You blind little fool." He bit off the words. "Don't you know why even now?"

She didn't. She simply stared at him, her blue eyes wide and clear and curious.

He groaned. "Meg!" He let out a long, rough breath and forcibly eased the grip of his lean hands and pushed her away. He shoved his hands into his pockets and stared for a long time into her wide, guileless eyes. "No, you don't understand, do you?" he said heavily. "I thought you might mature in New York." His eyes narrowed and he frowned. "What was that talk about some man wanting to keep you, then?"

She smiled sheepishly. "He's the caretaker of my apartment house. He wanted to adopt me."

"Good God!"

She rested her fingers on his arms, feeling their strength, loving them. She leaned against him gently with subdued delight that heightened when his hands came out of his pockets and smoothed over her shoulders. "There really isn't room in my life for complications," she said sadly. "Even with you. It wouldn't be wise." She forced a laugh from her tight throat. "Besides, I'm sure you have all the women you need already."

"Of course," he agreed with maddening carelessness and a curious watchfulness. "But I've wanted you for a very long time. We started something that we never finished. I want to get you out of my system, Meg, once and for all."

"Have you considered hiring an exorcist?" she asked, resorting to humor. She pushed playfully at his chest, feeling his heartbeat under her hands. "How about plastering a photo of me on one of your women...?''

He shook her gently. "Stop that."

"Besides," she said sighing and looping her arms around his neck, "I'd probably get pregnant and there'd be a scandal in the aircraft community. My career would be shot, your reputation would be ruined and we'd have a baby that neither of us wanted." Odd that the threat of pregnancy no longer terrified her, she thought idly.

"Mary Margaret, this is the twentieth century," he murmured on a laugh. "Women don't get pregnant these days unless they want to."

She turned her head slightly as she looked up at him, wide-eyed. "Why, Mr. Ryker, you sound so sophisticated. I suppose you keep a closetful of supplies?"

He burst out laughing. "Hell."

She smiled up at him. "Stop baiting me," she said. "I don't want to sleep with you and ruin a beautiful friendship. We've been friends for a long time, Steve, even if cautious ones."

"Friend, enemy, sparring partner," he agreed. The smile turned to a blank-faced stare with emotion suddenly glittering dangerously in his silver eyes. His chest rose and fell roughly and he moved a hand into the thick hair knotted at her nape and grasped it suddenly. He held her head firmly while he started to bend toward her.

"Steve..." she protested uncertainly.

"One kiss," he whispered back gruffly. "Is that so much to ask?"

"We shouldn't," she whispered at his lips.

"I know..." His hard mouth brushed over hers slowly, suggestively. His powerful body went very still and his free hand moved to her throat, stroking it tenderly. His thumb tugged at the lower lip that held stubbornly to its mate and broke the taut line.

Her hands pressed at his shirtfront, fascinated by warm, hard muscle and a heavy heartbeat. She couldn't quite manage to push him away.

"Mary Margaret," he breathed jerkily, and then he took her mouth.

"Oh, glory...!" she moaned, shivering. It was a jolt like diving into ice water. It burned through her body and through her veins and made her go rigid with helpless pleasure. He was far more expert than he'd been even four years ago. His tongue gently probed its way into the warm darkness of her mouth and she gasped at the darting, hungry pressure of its invasion. He tasted of smoke and mint, and his mouth was rough, as if he'd gone hungry for kisses.

While she was gathering up willpower to resist him, he reached down and lifted her in his hard arms, crushing her into the wall of his chest while his devouring kisses made her oblivious to everything except desire. At the center of the world was Steve and his hunger, and she was suddenly, shockingly, doing her very best to satisfy it, to satisfy him, with her arms clinging helplessly around his neck.

He lifted his mouth to draw in a ragged breath, and she hung there with swollen lips, wide-eyed, breathing like a distance runner.

"If you don't stop," she whispered unsteadily, "I'll tear your clothes off and ravish you right here on the carpet!"

Despite his staggering hunger, the humor broke through, as it always had with her, only with her. There had never been another woman who could make him laugh, could make him feel so alive.

"Oh, God, why can't you shut up for five minutes?" he managed through reluctant laughter.

"Self-defense," she said, laughing, too, her own voice breathless with traces of passion. "Oh, Steve, can you kiss!" she moaned.

He shook his head, defeated. He let her slide down his body to the floor, close enough to feel what had happened to him.

"Sorry," she murmured impishly.

"Only with you, honey," he said heavily, the endearment coming easily when he never used them. He held her arms firmly for a minute before he let her go with a rueful smile and turned away to light another cigarette. "Odd, that reaction. I need a little time with most women. It was never that way with you."

She hadn't thought about it in four years. Now she had to, and he was right. The minute he'd touched her, he'd been capable. She'd convinced herself that he never wanted her, but her memory hadn't dimmed enough to forget the size and power of him in arousal. She'd been a little afraid of him the first time it had happened, in fact, although he'd assured her that they were compatible in every way, especially in that one. She didn't like remembering how intimate they'd been, because it was still painful to remember how it had all ended. Looking back, it seemed impossible that he could have gone to Daphne after they argued, unless . . .

She stiffened as she remembered how desperately he'd wanted her. Had he been so desperate that he'd needed to spend his desire with someone else?

"Steve," she began.

He glanced at her. "What?"

"What you said, earlier. Was it difficult for you," she said slowly. "Holding back?"

"Yes." His face changed. "Apparently that didn't occur to you four years ago," he said sarcastically.

"A lot of things didn't occur to me four years ago," she said. She felt a dawning fear that she didn't want to explore.

"Don't strain your memory," he said with a mocking smile. "God forbid that you might have to reconsider your position. It's too damned late, even if you did."

"I know that. I wouldn't . . . I have my career."

"Your career." He nodded, but there was something disconcerting in the way he said it, in the way he looked at her.

"I'd better see about the roast," she murmured, retreating.

He studied her face with a purely masculine appreciation. "Better fix your lipstick, unless you want David making embarrassing remarks."

"David is terrified of me," she informed him. "I once beat him up in full view of half our classmates."

"So he told me, but he's grown."

"Not too much." She touched her mouth. It was faintly sore from the pressure of his hard kisses. She wouldn't have expected so much passion from him after four years.

"Did I hurt?" he asked quietly. "I didn't mean to."

"You always were a little rough when we made love," she recalled with a wistful smile. "I never minded."

His eyes kindled and before he could make the move his expression telegraphed, she beat a hasty retreat into the kitchen. He was overwhelming at close range, and she couldn't handle an affair with him. She didn't dare try. Having lived through losing him once, she knew she'd never survive having to go through it again. He still wanted her, but that was all. She was filed under unfinished business, and there was something a little disturbing about his attitude toward her. It wasn't quite unsatisfied passion on his part, she thought nervously. It was more like a deeply buried, long-nurtured vendetta.

It was probably a good thing that she was going back to New York soon, she thought dimly. And not a minute *too* soon. Her knees were so wobbly she could barely walk, and just from one kiss. If he turned up the heat, as he had during their time together, she would never be able to resist him. The needs she felt were overpowering now. She was a woman and she reacted like one. It was her bad luck that the only man who aroused her was the one man she daren't succumb to. If Steve really was holding a grudge against her for breaking off their engagement, giving in to him would be a recipe for disaster.

*   *   *

Supper was a rather quiet affair, with Meg intro-
spective and Steven taciturn while David tried to carry
the conversation alone.

"Can't you two say something? Just a word now
and again while I try to enjoy this perfectly cooked pot
roast?" David groaned, glancing from one set face to
the other. "Have you had another fight?"

"We haven't been fighting," Meg said innocently.
"Have we, Steve?"

Steven looked down at his plate, deliberately cutting a piece of meat without replying.

David threw up his hands. "I'll never understand
you two!" he muttered. "I'll just go see about dessert, shall I? I shall," he said, but he was talking to
himself as he left the room.

"I don't want any," she called after him.

"Yes, she does," Steve said immediately, catching
her eyes. "You're too thin. If you lose another two or
three pounds, you'll be able to walk through a harp."

"I'm a dancer," she said. "I can't dance with a fat
body."

He smiled gently. "That's right. Fight me." Something alien glittered in his eyes and his breathing
quickened.

"Somebody needs to," she said with forced humor. "All that feminine fawning has ruined you. Your
mother said that lines of women form everywhere you
go these days."

His eyes contemplated his coffee cup intensely and
his brow furrowed. "Did she?" he asked absently.

"But that you never take any of them seriously."
She laughed, but without much humor. "Haven't you even thought about marrying?"

He looked up, his expression briefly hostile. "Sure. Once."

She felt uncomfortable. "It wouldn't have worked," she said stiffly. "I wouldn't have shared you, even when I was eighteen and naive."

His eyes narrowed. "You think I'm modern enough in my outlook to keep a wife and a mistress at the same time?"

The question disturbed her. "Daphne was beautiful and sophisticated," she replied. "I was green behind the ears. Totally uninhibited. I used to embarrass you..."

"Never!"

There was muted violence in the explosive word.

She glanced up at him curiously. "But I did! Your father said that's why you never liked to take me out in public..."

"My father. What a champion." He lifted the cold coffee to his lips and sipped it. It felt as cold as he did inside. He looked at Meg and ached. "Between them, your mother and my father did a pretty damned good job, didn't they?"

"Daphne was a fact," she replied stubbornly.

He drew in a long, weary breath. "Yes. She was, wasn't she? You saw that for yourself in the newspaper."

"I certainly did." She sounded bitter. She hated having given her feelings away. She forced a smile. "But, as they say, no harm done. I have a bright career ahead of me and you're a millionaire several times over."

"I'm that, all right. I look in the mirror twice a day and say, 'lucky me.' "

"Don't tease."

He turned his wrist and glanced at the face of the thin gold watch. "I have to go," he said, pushing back his chair.

"Are you off to a business meeting?" she probed gently.

He stared at her without speaking for a few seconds, just long enough to give him a psychological advantage. "No," he said. "I have a date. As my mother told you," he added with a cold smile, "I don't have any problem getting women these days."

Meg didn't know how she managed to smile, but she did. "The lucky girl," she murmured on a prolonged sigh.

Steve glowered at her. "You never stop, do you?"

"Can I help it if you're devastating?" she replied. "I don't blame women for falling all over you. I used to."

"Not for long."

She searched his hard face curiously. "I should have talked to you about Daphne, instead of running away."

"Let the past lie," he said harshly. "We're not the same people we were."

"One of us certainly isn't," she mused dryly. "You never used to kiss me like that!"

He cocked an eyebrow. "Did you expect me to remain celibate when you defected?"

"Of course not," she replied, averting her eyes. "That would have been asking the impossible."

"Fidelity belongs to a committed relationship," he said.

She was looking at her hands, not at him. Life seemed so empty lately. Even dancing didn't fill the great hollow space in her heart. "Being in a committed relationship wouldn't have mattered," she murmured. "I doubt if you'd have been capable of staying faithful to just one woman, what with your track record and all. And I'm hardly a raving beauty like Daphne."

He stiffened slightly, but no reaction showed in his face. He watched her and glowered. "Nice try, but it doesn't work."

She glanced up, surprised. "What doesn't?"

"The wounded, downcast look," he said. He stretched, and muscles rippled under his knit shirt. "I know you too well, Meg," he added. "You always were theatrical."

She stared at him without blinking. "Would you have liked it if I'd gone raging to the door of your apartment after I saw you and Daphne pictured in that newspaper?"

His face hardened to stone. "No," he admitted, "I loathe scenes. All the same, there's no reason to lie about the reason you wanted to break our engagement. You told your mother that dancing was more important than me, that you got cold feet and ran for it. That's all she told me."

Meg was puzzled, but perhaps Nicole had decided against mentioning Daphne's place in Steven's life. "I suppose she decided that the best course all around was to make you believe my career was the reason I left.''

"That's right. Your *mother* decided," he corrected, and his eyes glittered coldly. "She yelled frog, and you jumped. You always were afraid of her."

"Who wasn't?" she muttered. "She was a worldbeater, and I was a sheltered babe in the woods. I didn't know beans about men until you came along."

"You still don't," he said flatly. "I'm surprised that living in New York hasn't changed you."

"What you are is what you are, despite where you live," she reminded him. She looked down again, infuriated with him. "I dance. That's what I do. That's all I do. I've worked hard all my life at ballet, and now I'm beginning to reap the rewards for it. I like my life. So it was probably a good thing that I found out how you felt about me in time, wasn't it? I had a lucky escape, Steve," she added bitterly.

He moved close, just close enough to make her feel threatened, to make her aware of him so that she'd look up.

He smiled with faint cruelty. "Does your good fortune compensate?" he asked with soft sarcasm.

"For what?"

"For knowing how much other women enjoy lying in my arms in the darkness."

She felt her composure shatter, and knew by the smile that he'd seen it in her eyes.

"Damn you!" she choked.

He turned away, laughing. "That's what I thought." He paused at the doorway. "Tell your brother I'll call him tomorrow." His eyes narrowed. "I hated you when your mother handed me the ring you'd left with her. You were the biggest mistake of my life. And, as you said, it was a lucky escape. For both of us."

He turned and left, his steady footsteps echoing down the hall before the door opened and closed with firm control behind him. Meg stood where he'd left her, aching from head to toe with renewed misery. He said he'd hated her in the past, but it was still there, in his eyes, when he looked at her. He hadn't stopped resenting her for what she'd done, despite the fact that he'd been unfaithful to her. He was in the wrong, so why was he blaming Meg?

"Where's Steve?" her brother asked when he reappeared.

"He had to go. He had a hot date," she said through her teeth.

"Good old Steve. He sure can draw 'em. I wish I had half his... Where are you going?"

"To bed," Meg said from the staircase, and her voice didn't encourage any more questions.

Meg only wished that she had someplace to go, but she was stuck in Wichita for the time being. Stuck with Steven always around, throwing his new conquests in her face. She limped because of the accident, and the tendons were mending, but not as quickly as she'd hoped. The doctor had been uncertain as to whether the damage would eventually right itself, and the physical therapist whom Meg saw three times a week was uncommunicative. Talk to the doctor, she told Meg. But Meg wouldn't, because she knew she wasn't making much progress and she was afraid to know why.

Besides her injury, there was no work in New York for her just now. Her ballet company couldn't perform without funds, and unless they raised some soon, she wouldn't have a job. It was a pity to waste so many years of her life on such a gamble. She loved ballet. If only she were wealthy enough to finance the company herself, but her small dividends from her stock in Ryker Air wouldn't be nearly enough.

David didn't have the money, either, but Steve did. She grimaced at just the thought. Steve would throw the money away or even burn it before he'd lend any to Meg. Not that she'd ever ask him, she promised herself. She had too much pride.

She'd tried not to panic at the thought of never dancing again. She consoled herself with a small dream of her own; of opening a ballet school here in Wichita. It would be nice to teach little girls how to dance. After all, Meg had studied ballet since her fourth birthday. She certainly had the knowledge, and she loved children. It was an option that she'd never seriously considered before, but now, with her injury, it became a security blanket. It was there to keep her going. If she failed in one area, she still had prospects in another. Yes, she had prospects.

*   *   *

The next morning, it was raining. Meg looked out
the front window and smiled wistfully, because the
rain pounding down on the sprouting grass and leaf-
ing trees suited her mood. It was late spring. There
were flowers blooming and, thank God, no tornadoes
looming with this shower. The rain was nice, if unex-
pected.

She did her exercises, glowering at the ankle that
was still stiff and painful after weeks of patient work.
David was at the office and no doubt so was Steve—if
he wasn't too worn out from the night before, she
thought furiously. How dare he rub his latest conquest in her face and make sarcastic and painful remarks about it?

He wasn't the person she'd known at eighteen. That
Steve had been a quiet man without the cruelty of this
new man who used women and tossed them aside. Or
perhaps he'd always been like this, except that Meg
had been looking at him through loving eyes and
missed all his flaws.

She didn't expect to see him again after his harsh-
ness the night before, but David telephoned just before he left the office with an invitation to dinner from
Steve.

"We've just signed a new contract with a Middle-
Eastern potentate. We're taking his representative out
for dinner and Steve wants you to come with us."

"Why me?" she asked with faint bitterness. "Am I
being offered as a treat to his client or is he thinking of
selling me into slavery on the Barbary Coast? I understand blondes are still much in demand there."

David didn't catch the bitterness in her voice. He laughed uproariously, covered the mouthpiece and mumbled something. "Steve says that's not a bad idea, and for you to wear a harem outfit."

"Tell him fat chance," she mumbled. "I don't know if I want to go. Surely Steven has plenty of women who could help him entertain his business friends."

"Don't be difficult," David chided. "A night out would do you good."

"All right. I'll be ready when you get home."

"Good."

She hung up, wondering why she'd given in. Steven had probably invited one of his women and was going to rub Meg's face in his latest conquest. She herself would no doubt be tossed to the Arab for dessert. Well, he was due for a surprise if he thought she'd go along with his plotting!

By the time David opened the front door, Meg was dressed in an outfit she'd bought for a Halloween party in New York: a black dress that covered her from just under her ears to her ankles, set off by a wide silver belt and silver-sprayed flat shoes. It was impossible to wear high heels just yet, and even though her limp wasn't pronounced, walking was difficult enough in flats. Her hair was in its neat bun and she wore no makeup. She didn't realize that her fair beauty made makeup superfluous anyway. She had an exquisitely creamy complexion with a natural blush all its own.

"Wow!" David whistled.

She glowered at him. "You aren't supposed to approve. I'm rebelling. This is a revolutionary outfit, not debutante dressing."

"I know that, and so will Steve. But—" he grinned as he took her arm and herded her out the door "—believe me, he'll approve."

Three

———

David's remark made sense until he escorted Meg into the restaurant where Steve—surprisingly without a woman in tow—and a tall, very dark Arab in an expensive European suit were seated. The men stood up as Meg and David approached. The Arab's gaze was approving. The puzzle pieces as to why Steve would be happy with her outfit fell into place.

"Remember that the Middle East isn't exactly liberated territory," David whispered. "You're dressed very correctly for this evening."

"Oh, boy," she muttered angrily. If she'd thought about it, she'd have worn her backless yellow gown....

"*Enchanté, mademoiselle,*" the foreigner said with lazy delight as he was introduced to her. He smiled and his black mustache twitched. He was incredibly hand-

some, with eyes that were large and almost a liquid
black. He was charming without being condescend-
ing or offensive. "You are a dancer, I believe? A ballerina?"

"Yes," Meg murmured demurely. She smiled at
him. "And you are the representative of your country?"

He quirked an eyebrow and glanced at Steve. "Indeed, I am."

"Do tell me about your part of the world," she said
with genuine interest, totally ignoring Steve and her
brother.

He did, to the exclusion of business, until Steve sat
glowering at her over dessert and coffee. She shifted a
little uncomfortably under that cold look, and Ahmed
suddenly noticed his business colleague.

He chuckled softly. "Steven, my friend, I digress.
Forgive me. But *mademoiselle* is such charming company that she chases all thought of business from my
poor mind."

"No harm done," Steve replied quietly.

"I'm sorry," Meg said genuinely. "I didn't mean to
distract you, but I do find your culture fascinating.
You're very well educated," Meg said.

He smiled. "Oxford, class of '82."

She sighed. "Perhaps I should have gone to college
instead of trying to study ballet."

"What a sad loss to the world of the arts if that had
been so, *mademoiselle*. Historians are many. Good
dancers, alas, are like diamonds."

Her cheeks flushed with flattery and excitement.

Steven's fingers closed around his fork and he stared at it. "About these new jets we're selling you, Ahmed," he persisted.

"Yes, we must discuss them. I have been led astray by a lovely face and a kind heart." He smiled at Meg. "But my duty will not allow me to divert my interests too radically from my purpose in coming here. You will forgive us if we turn our minds to the matter at hand, *mademoiselle?*"

"Of course," she replied softly.

"Kind of you," Steven murmured, his dagger glance saying much more than the polite words.

"For you, Steven, anything," she replied in kind.

The evening was both long and short. All too soon, David found himself accompanying the tall Arab back to his suite at the hotel while Steven appropriated Meg and eased her into the passenger seat of his Jaguar.

"Why is it always a Jaguar?" she asked curiously when he was inside and the engine was running.

"I like Jaguars."

"You would."

He pulled the sleek car out into traffic. "Leave Ahmed alone," he said without preamble.

"Ah. I'm being warned off." She nodded. "It's perfectly obvious that you consider me a woman of international intrigue, out to filch top-secret information and sell it to enemy agents." She frowned. "Who is the enemy these days, anyway?"

"Mata Hari, you aren't."

"Don't insult me. I have potential." She struck a pose, with her hand suspended behind her nape and her perfect facial profile toward him. "With a little careful tutoring, I could be devastating."

"With a little careful tutoring, you could be concealed in an oil drum and floated down the river to Oklahoma."

"You have no sense of humor."

He shrugged. "Not much to laugh about these days. Not in my life."

She leaned her cheek against the soft seat and watched him as he controlled the powerful car. It was odd that she always felt safe with him. Safe, and excited beyond words. Just looking at him made her tremble.

"What are you thinking?" he asked.

"That I'm sorry you never made love to me," she said without thinking.

The car swerved and his face tautened. He never looked at her. "Don't do that."

She drew in a slow breath, tracing patterns in the upholstery. "Aren't you, really?"

"You might have been addictive. I don't like addiction."

"That's why you smoke," she agreed, staring pointedly at the glowing cigarette in his lean, dark hand.

He did glance at her then, to glare. "I'm not addicted to nicotine. I can quit anytime I feel like it."

"What's wrong with right now?"

His dark eyes narrowed.

"What's wrong? Are you afraid you can't do without it?" she coaxed.

He pressed the power window switch, then threw the cigarette out when there was an opening. The window went back up again.

Meg grinned at him. "You'll be shaking in seconds," she predicted. "Combing the floor for old cigarette butts with a speck of tobacco left in them. Begging stubs from strangers."

"Unwise, Meg."

"What is? Taunting you?"

"I might decide to find another way to occupy my hands," he said suggestively.

She threw her arms out to the side and closed her eyes. "Go ahead!" she invited theatrically. "Ravish me!"

The car slammed to a halt and Meg's eyes opened as wide as cups. She stared at him, horrified.

He lifted an eyebrow as her arms clutched her breasts and a blush flamed on her face.

"Why, Meg, is anything wrong?" he asked pleasantly. "I just stopped to let the ambulance by."

"What amb—"

Sirens and flashing red lights swept past them and vanished quickly into the distance. Meg felt like sinking through the floorboard with embarrassment.

Steven's eyes narrowed just a little. He looped one long arm over the back of her seat and studied her in the darkened car.

"All bluff, aren't you?" he chided. "Didn't I warn you that playing games with me would get you into trouble?"

"Yes," she said. "But you've done nicely without me for four years."

He didn't answer. His hand lowered to her throat and he toyed with a wisp of her hair that had come loose from her bun, teasing her skin until her pulse began to race and her body grew hot in the tense silence.

"Steven, don't," she whispered huskily, staying his hand.

"Let me excite you, Meg," he replied quietly. He moved closer, easing her hand aside. His mouth poised over hers and he began all over again, teasing, touching, just at her throat while his coffee-scented breath came into her mouth and made her body ache. "It was like this the first night I took you out. Do you remember?" His voice was a deep, soft caress, and his hand made her shiver with its tender tracing. "I parked the car in your own driveway after we'd had dinner. I touched you, just like this, while we talked. You were more impulsive then, much less uninhibited. Do you remember what you did, Meg?"

She was finding it difficult to talk and breathe at the same time. "I was very... young," she said, defending herself.

"You were hungry." His lips parted and brushed her mouth open, softly nibbling at it until he heard the sound she made deep in her throat. "You unbuttoned my shirt and slid your hand inside it, right down to my waist."

She shivered, remembering what that had triggered. His mouth had hit hers like a tidal wave, with a groan that echoed in the silence of the car. He'd lifted her, turned her, and his hand had gone down inside the low bodice of her black dress to cup her naked breast. She'd come to her senses all too soon, fighting the intimacy. He'd stopped at once, and he'd smiled down at her as she lay panting in his arms, on fire with the first total desire she'd ever felt in her life. He'd known. Then, and now...

"You were so innocent," he said quietly, remembering. "You had no idea why I reacted so violently to such a little caress. It was like the first time I let you feel me against you when I was fully aroused. You were shocked and frightened."

"My parents never told me anything, and my girl-friends were just as stupid as I was, they made sure of it," she said hesitantly. "All the reading in the world doesn't prepare you for what happens, for what you feel when a man touches you intimately."

His hand smoothed over the shoulder of her black dress, back to the zipper. Slowly, gently, he eased it down, controlling her panicked movement with careless ease.

"It's been four years and you want it," he said. "You want me."

She couldn't believe that she was allowing him to do this! She felt like a zombie as he eased the fabric below the soft, lacy cup of her strapless bra and looked at her. His big, lean hand, darkly tanned, stroked her collarbone and down, smoothing over the swell of her breasts while he looked at her in the semidarkness.

His mouth touched her forehead. His breath was a little unsteady. So was hers.

"Let me unhook it, Meg. I want you in my mouth."

This had always been his sharpest weapon, this way of talking to her that made her body burn with dark, wicked desires. Her forehead rested against his chin while his fingers quickly disposed of three small hooks. She felt the cool air on her body even as he moved her back and looked down, his posture suddenly stiff and poised, controlled.

"My God." It was reverent, the way he spoke, the way he looked at her. His hands contracted on her shoulders as if he were afraid that she might vanish.

"I let you look at me . . . that last night," she whispered unsteadily. "And you went to her!"

"No. No," he whispered, bending his head. "No, Meg!"

His mouth fastened on her taut nipple and he groaned as he lifted her, turned her, suckling her in a silence that blazed with tension and promise.

Her fingers gripped his thick hair and held on while his mouth gave her the most intense pleasure she'd ever known. He'd tried to kiss her this way that long-ago night and she'd fought him. It had been too much for her already overloaded senses and, coupled with his raging arousal and the sudden determination of his weight on her body, she'd panicked. But she was older now, with four years of abstinence to heighten her need, strip her nerves raw. She was starved for him.

His mouth fed on her while his fingers traced around the firm softness he was enjoying. She felt his tongue, his teeth, the slow suction that seemed to draw the heart right out of her body. She shuddered, helpless, anguished, as the ardent pressure of his mouth only made the hunger grow.

He felt her tremble and slowly lifted his head.

"Noo...!" She choked, clutching at him, trying to draw his mouth back to her body. "Steve... please... please!"

He drew her face into his throat and held her, his arms punishing, his breath as ragged as her own.

"Please!" she sobbed, clinging.

"Here...!" He fought the buttons of his shirt open and dragged her inside it, pressing her close to him, so that her bare breasts were rubbing against the thick hair on his chest, teasing his tense muscles. "Meg," he breathed tenderly. "Oh, Meg, Meg...!" His hands found their way around her, sweeping down her bare back in long, hungry caresses that made the intimacy even more dangerous, more threatening.

Her mouth pressed soft kisses into his throat, his neck, his collarbone, and she felt the need like a knife.

He turned her head and kissed her again, a long, slow, deep kiss that never seemed to end while around them the night darkened and the wind blew.

Somewhere in the middle of it, she began to cry; great, broken sobs of guilt and grief and unappeased hunger. He held her, cradled her against him, his eyes as anguished as his unsatisfied body. But slowly, finally, the desire in both of them began to relax.

"Don't cry," he whispered, kissing the tears from her eyes. "It was inevitable."

She turned her face so that he could kiss the other side of it, her eyes closed while she savored the rare, exquisite tenderness.

When she felt his lips reluctantly draw away, she opened her eyes and looked into his. They were soft, just for her, just for the moment. Soft and hungry, and somehow violent.

"You're untouched," he said huskily, his face setting into hard, familiar lines. "Even here." His hand smoothed over her bare, swollen breast and as if the feel of it drove him mad, he bent his head and tenderly drew his lips over it, breathing in the scent of her body. "Totally, absolutely untouched."

"I...can't feel like this with any other man," she confessed, shaken to her soul by what they were sharing. "I can't bear another man's eyes to touch me, much less his hands."

His breath drew in raggedly. "Why in God's name did you leave, damn you?"

"I was afraid!"

"Of this?" His mouth opened over her nipple and she cried out at the flash of pleasure it gave her to feel it so intimately.

"I was a virgin," she gasped.

"You still are." He drew her across him, one big hand gathering her hips blatantly into the hard thrust of his, holding her there while he searched her eyes. "And you're still afraid," he said finally, watching the shocked apprehension grow on her face. "Terrified of intimacy with me."

She swallowed, then swallowed again. Her eyes dropped to his bare chest. "Not...of that."

"Then what?"

His body throbbed. She could feel the heat and power of it and she felt faint with the knowledge of how desperately he wanted her. "Steven, my sister died in childbirth."

"Yes, I know. Your father told me. It was such a private thing, I didn't feel it was my place to ask questions. I just know she was twelve years older than you."

She looked up at him. "She was...like me," she whispered slowly. "Thin and slender, not very big in the hips at all. They lived up north. It snowed six feet the winter she was ready to deliver and her husband couldn't get her to a hospital in time. She died. So did the baby." Meg hesitated, nibbling her lower lip. "Childbirth is difficult for the women in my family. My mother had to have a cesarean section when I was born. I was very sheltered and after my sister died, mother made it sound as if pregnancy would be a death sentence for me, too. She made me terrified of getting pregnant," she added miserably, hiding her face from him.

He eased his intimate hold on her, stunned. His hand guided her cheek to his broad, hair-roughened chest and he held her there, letting her feel the heat of his body, the heavy slam of his heart under her ear.

"We never discussed this."

"I was very young, as you said," she replied, closing her eyes. "I couldn't tell you. It was so intimate a thing to say, and I was already overwhelmed by you physically. Every time you touched me, I went light-headed and hot and shaky all over." Her eyes closed. "I still do."

His fingers tangled gently in her hair, comforting now instead of arousing. "I could have reassured you, if you'd only told me."

"Perhaps." She nuzzled her cheek against him. "But I had terrors of getting pregnant, and you came on very strong that night. The argument...seemed like a reprieve at the time. You told me to get out, and then you took Daphne to a public place so that it would be in all the papers. I told myself that choosing dancing made more sense than choosing you. It made it easier to go away."

He lifted his head, staring out the darkened window. Seconds later, he looked down at her, his eyes lingering on her breasts.

She smiled sadly. "You don't believe me, do you? You're still bitter, Steven."

"You don't think I'm entitled to be?"

She shifted against him, her eyes adoring his hard face, totally at peace with him even in this intimacy now. "I didn't think you cared enough to be hurt."

"I didn't," he agreed readily. "But my pride took a few blows."

"Nicole said you got drunk..."

He smiled cruelly. "Did she add that I was with Daphne at the time?"

She stiffened, hating him.

His warm hand covered her breast blatantly, feeling her heartbeat race even through her anger. He searched her eyes. "I still want you," he said flatly. "More than ever."

She knew it. His face was alive with desire. "It wouldn't be wise," she said quietly. "As you once said, Steven, addictions are best avoided."

"You flatter yourself if you think I'm crazy enough to become addicted to you again," he said with a faintly mocking smile as all the anguish of those four years sat on him.

Meg was arrested by his expression. The mention of the past seemed to have brought all the bitterness back, all the anger. She didn't know what to say. "Steven . . ."

His hand pressed closer, warm against her bare skin in the faint chill of the car. "Your ballet company needs money. All right, Meg," he said softly. "I'll get you out of the hole."

"You will!" she exclaimed.

"Oh, yes. I'll be your company angel. But there's a price."

His voice was too silky. She felt the apprehension as if it were tangible. "What is the price?" she asked.

"Can't you figure it out?" he asked with faint hauteur in his smile. "Then I'll tell you. Sleep with me. Give me one night, Meg, to get you out of my system. And in return, I'll give you back your precious dancing."

Four

———

Meg spent a long, sleepless night agonizing over Steven's proposal. She couldn't really believe that he'd said such a thing, or that he'd actually expected her to agree. How could his feverish ardor have turned to contempt in so short a time? It must be as she thought: he wanted nothing more than revenge because she'd run out on him. Even her explanation had fallen on deaf ears. Or perhaps he hadn't wanted to believe it. And hadn't he been just as much at fault, after all? He was the one who'd sent her away. He'd told her to get out of his life.

She wished now that she'd reminded him of that fact more forcibly. But his slowly drawled insult had made her forget everything. She'd torn out of his arms, putting her clothes to rights with trembling hands while he laughed harshly at her efforts.

"That was cruel, Steven," she'd said hoarsely, glaring at him when she was finally presentable again.

"Really? In fact, I meant it," he added. "And the offer still stands. Sleep with me and I'll drag your precious company back from the brink. You won't have to worry about pregnancy, either," he added as he started the car. "I'll protect you from it with my last breath. You see, Meg, the last thing in the world I want now is to be tied to you by a child." His eyes had punctuated the insult, going slowly over her body as if he could see under her clothes. "All I want is for this madness to be over, once and for all."

As if it ever would be, she thought suddenly, when he'd left her at her door without a word and drove off. The madness, as he called it, was going to be permanent, because she'd taken the easy way out four years ago. She hadn't confessed her fears and misgivings about intimacy with him, or challenged him about Daphne. She'd been afraid to say what she thought, even more afraid to fight for his love. Instead, she'd listened to others—his father and her own mother, who'd wanted Meg to have a career in ballet and never risk pregnancy at all.

But Steven's motives were even less clear. She'd often thought secretly that Steven was rather cold in any emotional way, that perhaps he'd been relieved when their engagement ended. His very courtship of her had been reluctant, forced, as if it was totally against his better judgment. Meg had thought at the time that love was something he would never understand completely. He had so little of it in his own life. His father had wanted a puppet that he could control. His mother had withdrawn from him when he was still a child, unable to understand his tempestuous nature much less cope with his hardheaded determination in all things.

Steven had grown up a loner. He still was. He might use a woman to ease his masculine hungers, but he avoided emotional closeness. Meg had sensed that, even at the age of eighteen. In a way, it was Steven's very detachment that she'd run from. She had the wisdom to know that her love for him and his desire for her would never make a relationship. And at the back of her mind, always in those days, was her unrealistic fear of childbirth. She wondered now if her mother hadn't deliberately cultivated that fear, to force Meg into line. Her mother had been a major manipulator. Just like Steven's father.

Meg had gone quickly upstairs the night before, calling a cheerful good-night to her brother, who was watching a late movie in the living room. She held up very well until she got into her own room, and then the angry tears washed down from her eyes.

A night of love in return for financing. Did he really think she held herself so cheaply? Well, Steven could hold his breath until she asked him for financial help, she thought furiously! The ballet company would manage somehow. She wouldn't meet his unreasonable terms, not even to save her career.

By the time Meg was up and moving around the next morning, David had already gone to the office.

She had a headache and a very sore ankle from just the small amount of walking she'd done the night before. She couldn't quite meet her own eyes in the mirror, though, remembering how easily she'd surrendered to Steven's hot ardor. She had no resistance when she got within a foot of him.

She washed her face, brushed her teeth and ate breakfast. She went to the hospital for her physical therapy and then came back home and did stretches for several minutes. All the while, she thought of Steven and how explosive their passion had been. It didn't help her mood.

David came home looking disturbed.

"Why so glum?" Meg teased gently.

He glanced at her. "What? Oh, there's nothing," he said quickly, and smiled. "If you haven't cooked anything, suppose we go out for a nice steak supper?"

Her eyebrows arched. "Steak?"

"Steak. I feel like chewing something."

"Ouch. Bad day?" she murmured.

"Vicious!" He shrugged. "By the way, Ahmed said that he'd like to join us, if you don't mind."

"Certainly not!" she said, smiling. "I like him."

"So do I. But don't get too attached to him," he cautioned. "There are some things going on that you don't know about, that you're safer not knowing about. But Ahmed isn't quite what he seems."

"Really?" She was intrigued. "Tell me more."

"You'll have to take my word for it," he said. "I'm not risking any more scathing comments from the boss. He was out for blood today. One of the secretaries threw a desk lamp at him and walked out of the building without severance pay!"

Meg's eyebrows arched. "Steven's secretary?"

"As a matter of fact, yes." He chuckled. "Everybody else ran for cover. Not Daphne. I suppose she'd known him for so long that she can handle him."

Meg's heart stopped beating. "Daphne—*the* Daphne he was sleeping with when he and I got engaged?"

David's eyes narrowed. "I don't think they were that intimate, and certainly not after he asked you to marry him. But, yes, they've known each other for years."

"I see."

"She was the reason you argued with him. The reason you left, as I remember."

She took a deep breath. "Part of it," she replied, correcting him. She forced a smile. "Actually she did a good turn. I'd never have had the opportunity to continue my training in New York if I'd married Steven, would I?"

"You haven't let a man near you since you left Wichita," David said sagely. "And don't tell me it's due to lack of time for a social life."

She lifted her chin. "Maybe Steve's an impossible act to follow," she said with an enigmatic smile. "Or maybe he taught me a bitter lesson about male loyalty."

"Steven's not what he seems," he said suddenly. "He's got a soft center, despite all that turmoil he creates. He was deeply hurt when you left. I don't think he ever got over you, Meg."

"His pride didn't, he even admitted it," she agreed. "But he never loved me. If he had, how could he have gone to Daphne?"

"Men do strange things when they feel threatened."

"I never threatened him," she muttered.

"No?" He stuck his hands into his pockets and studied her averted face. "Meg, in all the years we've known the Rykers, Steve never took a woman around for more than two weeks. He avoided any talk of involvement or marriage. Then he took you out one time and started talking about engagement rings."

"I was a novelty." She bit off the words.

"You were, indeed. You melted right through that wall of ice around him and made him laugh, made him young. Meg, if you'd ever really looked at him, you'd have seen how much he changed when he was with you. Steven Ryker would have thrown himself under a bus if you'd asked him to. He would have done anything for you. Anything," he added quietly. "His father didn't want Steven to marry you because he thought Steve was besotted enough to side with you in a proxy fight." He smiled at her shocked expression. "Don't you see that everyone was manipulating you for their own gain? You and Steven never had a chance, Meg. You fell right into line and did exactly what you were meant to do. And the one who really paid the price was poor old Steven, in love for the first time in his life."

"He didn't love me," she choked.

"That's true. He worshiped you. He couldn't take his eyes off you. Everything he did for that one long month you were engaged was designed solely to please you, every thought he had was for your comfort, your happiness." He shook his head. "You were too young to realize it, weren't you?"

She felt as if her legs wouldn't hold her. She sat down, heavily. "He never said a word."

"What could he have said? He isn't the type to beg. You left. He assumed you considered him expendable. He got drunk. Roaring drunk. He stayed that way for three days. Then he went back to work with a vengeance and started making money hand over fist. That's when the women started showing up, one after another. They numbed the ache, but he was still hurting. There was nothing anyone could do for him, except watch him suffer and pretend not to notice that he flinched whenever your name was mentioned."

She covered her face with her hands.

He laid a comforting hand on her shoulder. "Don't torture yourself. He did, finally, get over you, Meg. It took him a year and when he got through it, he was a better man. But he's not the same man. He's lost and gained something in the process. It's hardened him to emotion."

"I was an idiot," she said heavily, pushing back her loosened hair. "I loved him so much, but I was afraid of him. He seemed so distant sometimes, as if he couldn't bear to talk to me about anything personal."

"You were the same way," he prompted.

She smiled wistfully. "Of course I was. I was hopelessly repressed and introverted, and I couldn't believe that a man who was such a man wanted to marry me. I stood in awe of him then. I still do, a little. But now I understand him so much better . . . now that it's too late.''

"Are you sure that it is?"

She thought about the night before, about his exquisite ardor and then the pain and grief of hearing him proposition her. She nodded slowly. "Yes, David," she said, lifting pain-filled blue eyes to his. "I'm afraid so."

"I'm sorry."

She got to her feet. "Don't they say that things always work out for the best?" She smoothed her skirt. "Where are we going to eat?"

"Castello's. And I'm sorry to have to tell you that so is Steve."

She hated the thought of facing him, but she was no coward. She only shrugged fatalistically. "I'll get dressed, then."

He told her what time they needed to leave and went off to make a last-minute phone call.

Meg went upstairs. "I think I'll wear something red," she murmured angrily to herself. "With a V-neck, cut to the ankles in front, and with slits up both sides . . ."

She didn't have anything quite that revealing, but the red dress she pulled out of its neat wrapper had spaghetti straps and fringe. It was close-fitting, seductive. She left her blond hair down around her shoulders and used much more makeup than she normally did. She had some jewelry left over from the old

days, with diamonds. She got it out of the safe and
wore it, too. The song about going out in a blaze of
glory revolved in her mind. She was going to give
Steven Ryker hell.

As David had said, he was, indeed, in the restaurant. But he wasn't alone. And Meg's poor heart took
a dive when she saw who was with him: a slinky, sul-
try platinum blonde with a smooth tan, wearing a
black dress that probably cost twice what Meg's had.
It was Daphne, of course, draped against Steve's arm
as if she were an expensive piece of lint. Meg forced a
brilliant smile as Ahmed rose from the table, in a dis-
tinguished dark suit, and smiled with pure appreciation as she and David approached.

"Mademoiselle prompts me to indiscretion," he
said, taking her hand and bowing over it before he
kissed the knuckles in a very continental way. "I will
bite my tongue and subdue the words that tease my
mouth."

Meg laughed with delight. "If you intend asking me
to join your harem," she returned impishly, "you'll
have to wait until I'm too old to dance, I'm afraid."

"I am devastated," he said heavily.

Steven was staring at her, his silver eyes dangerous.
"What an interesting choice of color, Meg," he murmured.

She curtsied, grimacing as she made her injured
ankle throb with the action. "It's my favorite. Don't
you think it suits me?" she asked with a challenge in
her eyes.

He averted his gaze as if the words had shamed him.
"No, I don't," he said stiffly. "Sit down, David."

David helped Meg into the chair next to Ahmed and greeted Daphne.

"How did you manage this?" David asked the other woman.

"He likes having things thrown at him, don't you, Steven, darling?" Daphne laughed. "I got rehired at a higher salary. You should try it yourself."

"No, thanks." David sighed. "I'd be frog-marched to the elevator shaft for my pains."

"I don't suppose Meg is the type to throw things, are you, dear?" Daphne asked.

"Shall we find out?" Meg replied, lifting her water glass with a meaningful glance in Daphne's direction.

David put a hand on her wrist, shocked by her reaction.

"Forgive me if I've offended you," Daphne said quickly. She looked more than a little surprised herself. "Heavens, I just open my mouth and words fall out, I suppose," she added with a nervous, apologetic glance toward Steven.

Steven was frowning and his eyes never left Meg's.

"No need to apologize," Meg said stiffly. "I rarely take offense, even when people blatantly insult me."

Steven looked uncomfortable and the atmosphere at the table grew tense.

Ahmed stood up, holding his hand out to Meg. "I would be honored to have you dance with me," he offered.

"I would be honored to accept." Meg avoided Steven's eyes as she stood up and let Ahmed lead her onto the dance floor.

He held her very correctly. She liked the clean scent of him and the handsome face with liquid black eyes that smiled down at her. But there was no spark when he touched her, no throbbing ache to possess and be possessed.

"Thank you," she said quietly. "I think you saved the evening."

"Daphne has no malice in her, despite what you may think," he said gently. "It is quite obvious what Steven feels for you."

Meg flushed, letting her eyes fall to his white shirt. "Is it?"

"This dancing . . . it hurts you?" he asked suddenly when she was less than graceful and fell heavily against him.

She swallowed. "My ankle is still painful," she said honestly. "And not mending as I had hoped." Her eyes lifted with panic in their depths. "It was a bad sprain . . ."

"And dancing is your life."

She gnawed on her lower lip, wincing as she moved again with him to the bluesy music. "It has had to be," she said oddly.

"May I cut in?"

The voice was deep and cutting and not the kind to ignore unless a brawl was desirable.

"But of course," Ahmed said, smiling at Steven. *"Merci, mademoiselle,"* he added softly and moved back.

Steven drew Meg to him, much too closely, and riveted her in place with one long, powerful arm as he moved her to the music.

"My ankle hurts," she said icily, "and I don't want to dance with you."

"I know." He tilted her face up to his and studied the dark circles under her eyes, the wan complexion. "I know why you wore the red dress, too. It was to rub my nose in what I said to you last night, wasn't it?"

"Bingo," she said with a cold smile.

He drew in a long breath. His silver eyes slid over the length of her waving hair, down to her bare shoulders. They fell to her breasts where the soft V at the neckline revealed their exquisite swell, and his jaw clenched. The arm of her back went rigid.

"You have the softest skin I've ever touched," he said gruffly. "Silky and warm and fragrant. I don't need this dress to remind me that I can't think sanely when you're within reach."

"Then stay out of reach," she shot back. "Why don't you take Daphne home with you and seduce her? If you didn't on the way here," she added with hauteur.

She missed a step and he caught her, easily, holding her upright.

"That ankle is hurting you. You shouldn't be dancing," he said firmly.

"The therapist said to exercise it," she said through her teeth. "And she said that it would hurt."

He didn't say what he was thinking. If the ankle was painful after five long weeks, how would she be able to dance on it? Would it hold her weight? It certainly didn't seem as if it would.

She saw the expression on his face. "I'll dance again," she told him. "I will!"

He touched her face with lean, careful fingers, traced her cheek and her chin and around her full, bow mouth. "For yourself, Meg, or because it was what your mother always wanted?"

"It was the only thing I ever did in my life that pleased her," she said without thinking.

"Yes. I think perhaps it was." His finger traced her lower lip. Odd how tremulous that finger seemed, especially when it teased between her lips and felt them part, felt her breath catch. "Are you still afraid of making a baby?" he whispered unsteadily.

"Steven!" she exclaimed. She jerked her face back and it flushed red.

"You made me think about what happened that last night we were together before we fought," he said, as if she hadn't reacted to the question at all. "I remember when you started fighting me. I remember what I said to you."

"This isn't necessary . . . !" she broke in frantically.

"I said that if we went all the way, it wouldn't really matter," he whispered deeply, holding her eyes. "Because I'd love making you pregnant."

She actually shivered and her body trembled as it sought the strength and comfort of his.

He cradled her in his arms, barely moving to the music, his mouth at her ear. "You didn't think I was going to stop. And you were afraid of a baby."

"Yes."

His fingers threaded into her soft, silky hair and he drew her even closer. His legs trembled against her own as the incredible chemistry they shared made him weak. And all at once, instantly, he was fully capable and she could feel it.

"Don't pull away from me," he said roughly. "I know it repulses you, but, my God, it isn't as if I can help it ...!"

She stilled instantly. "Oh, no, it isn't that," she whispered, lifting her eyes. "I don't want to hurt you! You used to tell me not to move when it happened, remember?"

He stopped dancing and his eyes searched hers so hungrily that she could hardly bear the intensity of the look they were sharing.

His lips parted as he tried to breathe, enmeshed by his hunger for her, by the beauty of her uplifted face, the temptation of her perfect, innocent body against his. "I remember everything," he said tautly. "You haunt me, Meg. Night after empty night."

She saw the strain in his dark face and felt guilty that she should be the cause of it. Her hand pressed flat against his shirtfront, feeling the strength and heat and under it the feverish throb of his pulse.

"I'm sorry," she said tenderly. "I'm so sorry ..."

He fought for control, his eyes lifting finally to stare over her head.

Meg moved away a little, and began talking quite calmly about the state of the world, the weather, dancing lazily while he recovered.

"I have to stop now, Steven," she said finally. "My ankle really hurts."

He stopped dancing. His eyes searched over her face. "I'm sorry about what I said to you last night, when I asked you," he said curtly. "I wanted you to the point of madness." He laughed bitterly. "That, at least, has never changed."

Her eyes adored him. She couldn't help it. He was more perfect to her than anything in the world, and when he was close to her, she had everything. But what he wanted would destroy her.

"I can't sleep with you and just... just go on with my life," she said softly. "It would be another night, another body, to you. But it would be devastating to me. Not only my first time, but with someone whom I..." She averted her eyes. "Someone for whom I once cared very much."

"Look at me."

She forced her eyes up to his, curious about their sudden intent scrutiny.

"Meg," he said, as the music began again, "it wouldn't be just another night and another body."

"It would be for revenge," she argued. "And you know it, Steven. It isn't about lovemaking, it's about getting even. I walked out of your life and hurt you. Now you want to pay me back, and what better way than to sleep with me and walk away yourself?"

"Do you think I could?" he asked with a bitter laugh.

"Neither of us would really know until it happened." She stared at his chest. "I know you'd try to protect me, but you aren't quite in control when we make love. You certainly weren't last night." She raised her face. "Then what would we do if I really did get pregnant?"

His lips parted. He studied her slowly. "You could marry me," he said softly. "We could raise our child together."

The thought thrilled, uplifted, frightened. "And my career?"

The pleasure washed out of him. His face lost its softness and his eyes grew cold. "That, of course, would be history. And you couldn't stand that. After all, you've worked all your life for it, haven't you?" He let her go. "We'd better go back to the table. We don't want to put that ankle at risk."

They did go back to the table. He took Daphne's hand and kept it in his for the rest of the evening. And every time he looked at Meg, his eyes were hostile and full of bitterness and contempt.

Five

David and Meg, who'd taken a cab to the restaurant, rode back to their house with Ahmed in his chauffeured limousine. Steven, Meg noticed, hadn't even offered them a ride; he probably had other plans, ones that included Daphne.

"It's been a great evening," David remarked. "How much longer are you going to stay in Wichita, Ahmed?"

"Until the last of the authorizations are signed," the other man replied. He glanced at Meg with slow, bold appraisal in his liquid black eyes. "Alas, then duty forces me back to my own land. Are you certain that you would not consider coming with me, *ma chou?*" he teased. "You could wear that dress and enchant me as you dance."

Meg forced a smile, but she was having some misgivings about her future. Her ankle was no stronger than when it was first damaged. Her concern grew by the day.

"I'm very flattered," she began.

"We are allowing our women more freedom," he mused. "At least they are no longer required to wear veiling from head to toe and cover their faces in public."

"Are you married?" she asked curiously. "Aren't Moslems allowed four wives?"

The laughter went out of his eyes. "No, I am not married. It is true that a Moslem may have up to four wives, but while I accept many of the teachings of the Prophet, I am not Moslem, *mademoiselle*. I was raised a Christian, which precludes me from polygamy."

"That's the road, just up ahead," David said quickly, gesturing toward their street. "You haven't seen our home, have you, Ahmed?" he added, smiling at the other man.

"No."

"Do come in," Meg asked. "We can offer you coffee. Your chauffeur as well."

"Another time, perhaps," Ahmed said gently, glancing behind them at a dark car in the near distance. "I have an appointment this evening at my hotel."

"Certainly," Meg replied.

"Thanks for the ride. I'll see you tomorrow, then," David said as they pulled up in the driveway.

Ahmed nodded. "Friday will see the conclusion of our business," he remarked. "I should enjoy escorting the two of you and our friend Steven to a performance at the theater. I have obtained tickets in anticipation of your acceptance."

Meg was thrilled. "I'd love to! David...?"

"Certainly," her brother said readily. He smiled. "Thank you."

"I will send the car for you at six, then. We will enjoy a leisurely meal before the curtain rises." He didn't offer to get out of the car, but he smiled and waved at Meg as David closed the door behind her. The limousine sped off, with the dark car close behind it.

"Is he being followed?" she asked David carefully.

"Yes, he is," David said, but he avoided looking at her. "He has his own security people."

"I like him," she said as they walked toward the front door.

David glanced at her. "You've been very quiet since you danced with Steve," he observed. "More trouble?"

She sighed wistfully. "Not really. Steven's only shoving Daphne down my throat. Why should that bother me?"

"Maybe he's trying to make you jealous."

"That will be the day, when Steven Ryker stoops to that sort of tactic."

David started to speak and decided against it. He only smiled as he unlocked the door and let her in.

"Ahmed is very mysterious," she said abruptly. "It's as if he's not really what he seems at all. He's a very gentle man, isn't he?" she added thoughtfully.

He gave her a blank stare. "Ahmed? Uh, well, yes. Certainly. I mean, of course he is." He looked as if he had to bite his tongue. "But, despite the fact that Ahmed is Christian, he's still very much an Arab in his customs and beliefs. And his country is a hotbed of intrigue and danger right now." He studied her closely. "You don't watch much television, do you, Meg? Not the national news programs, I mean."

"They're much too upsetting for me," she confessed. "No, I don't watch the news or read newspapers unless I can't avoid them. I know," she said before he could taunt her about it, "I'm hiding my head in the sand. But honestly, David, what could I do to change any of that? We elect politicians and trust them to have our best interests at heart. It isn't the best system going, but I can hardly rush overseas and tell people to do what I think they should, now can I?"

"It doesn't hurt to stay informed," he said. "Although right now, maybe it's just as well that you aren't," he added under his breath. "See you in the morning."

"Yes." She stared after him, frowning. David could be pretty mysterious himself at times.

David didn't invite Steve to the house that week, because he could see how any mention of the man cut Meg. But although Wichita was a big city, it was still possible to run into people when you traveled in the same social circles.

Meg found it out the hard way when she went to a men's department store that her family had always frequented to buy a birthday present for David. She ran almost literally into Steve there.

If she was shocked and displeased to meet him, the reverse was also true. He looked instantly hostile.

Her eyes slid away from his tall, fit body in the pale tan suit he was wearing. It hurt to look at him too much.

"Shopping for a suit?" he asked sarcastically. "You'll have a hard time finding anything to fit you here."

"I'm shopping for David's birthday next week," she said tightly.

"By an odd coincidence, so am I."

"Doesn't your *secretary*," she stressed the word, "perform that sort of menial chore for you?"

"I pick out gifts for my friends myself," he said with cold hauteur. "Besides," he added, watching her face, "I have other uses for Daphne. I wouldn't want to tire her too much in the daytime."

Insinuating that he wanted her rested at night. Meg had to fight down anger and distaste. She kept her eyes on the ties. "Certainly not," she said with forced humor.

"My father was right in the first place," he said shortly, angered at her lack of reaction. "She would have made the perfect wife. I don't know why it took me four years to realize it."

Her heart died. *Died!* She swallowed. "Sometimes we don't realize the value of things until it's too late."

His breath caught, not quite audibly. "Don't we?"

She looked up, her eyes full of blue malice. "I didn't realize how much ballet meant to me until I got engaged to you," she said with a cold smile.

His fists clenched. He fought for control and smiled. "As we said once before, we had a lucky escape." He cocked his head and studied her. "How's the financing going for the ballet company?" he added pointedly.

She drew in a sharp breath. "Just fine, thanks," she said venomously. "I won't need any... help."

"Pity," he said, letting his eyes punctuate the word.

"Is it? I'm sure Daphne wouldn't agree!"

"Oh, she doesn't expect me to be faithful at this stage of the game," he replied lazily. "Not until the engagement's official, at least."

Meg felt faint. She knew the color was draining slowly out of her face, but she stood firm and didn't grab for support. "I see."

"I still have your ring," he said conversationally. "Locked up tight in my safe."

She remembered giving it to her mother to hand back to him. The memory was vivid, violent. Daphne. Daphne!

"I kept it to remind me what a fool I was to think I could make a wife of you," he continued. "I won't make the same mistake again. Daphne doesn't want just a career. She wants my babies," he added flatly, cruelly.

She dropped her eyes, exhausted, almost ill with the pain of what he was saying. Her hand trembled as she fingered a silk tie. "Ahmed invited us to dinner and the theater Friday night." Her voice only wobbled a little, thank God.

"I know," he said, and sounded unhappy about it.

She forced her eyes up. "You don't have to be deliberately insulting, do you, Steven?" she asked quietly. "I know you hate me. There's no need for all this—" She stopped, almost choking on the word that almost escaped.

"Isn't there? But, then, you don't know how I feel, do you, Meg? You never did. You never gave a damn, either." He shoved his hands deep into his pockets and glowered at her. She looked fragile somehow in the pale green knit suit she was wearing. "Ahmed is leaving soon," he told her. "Don't get attached to him."

"He's a friend. That's all."

His silver eyes slid over her bowed head with faint hunger and then moved away quickly. "How are the exercises coming?"

"Fine, thanks."

He hesitated, bristling with bad temper. "When do you leave?" he asked bluntly.

She didn't react. "At the end of the month."

He let out a breath. "Well, thank God for that!"

Her eyes closed briefly. She'd had enough. She pulled the tie she'd been examining off the rack and moved away, refusing to look at him, to speak to him. Her throat felt swollen, raw.

"I'll have this one, please," she told the smiling clerk and produced her credit card. Her voice sounded odd.

Steven was standing just behind her, trying desperately to work up to an apology. It was becoming a habit to savage her. All he could think about was how much he'd loved her, and how easily she'd discarded him. He didn't trust her, but, God, he still wanted her.

She colored his dreams. Without her, everything was flat. Even now, looking at her fed his heart, uplifted him. She was so lovely. Fair and sweet and gentle, and all she wanted was a pair of toe shoes and a stage.

He groaned inwardly. How was he going to survive when she left again? He never should have touched her. Now it was going to be just as bad as before. He was going to watch her walk away a second time and part of him was going to die.

Daphne was coming with him tonight or he didn't think he could survive Meg's company. Thank God for Daphne. She was a friend, and quite content to be that, but she was his co-conspirator as well now, part of this dangerous business that revolved around Ahmed. She was privileged to know things that no one else in his organization knew. But meanwhile she was also his camouflage. Daphne had a man of her own, one of the two government agents who were helping keep a careful eye on Ahmed. But fortunately, Meg didn't know that.

Steven was in some danger. Almost as much as Ahmed. He couldn't tell Meg that without having to give some top-secret answers. Daphne knew, of course. She was as protected as he was, as Ahmed was. But despite his bitterness toward Meg, he didn't want her in the line of fire. Loving her was a disease, he sometimes thought, and there was no cure, not even a temporary respite. She was the very blood in his veins. And to her, he was expendable. He was of no importance to her, because all she needed from life was to dance. The knowledge cut deep into his heart. It made him cruel. But hurting her gave him no pleasure. He watched her with possessive eyes, aching to hold her and apologize for his latest cruelty.

Her purchase completed, Meg left the counter and turned away without looking up. Steven, impelled by forces too strong to control, gently took her arm and pulled her with him to a secluded spot behind some suits.

He looked down into her surprised, wounded eyes until his body began to throb. "I keep hurting you, don't I?" he said roughly. "I don't mean to. Honest to God, I don't mean to, Meg!"

"Don't you?" she asked with a sad, weary smile. "It's all right, Steve," she said quietly, averting her eyes. "Heaven knows, you're entitled, after what I did to you!"

She pulled away from him and walked quickly out of the store, the cars and people blurring in front of her eyes.

Steve cursed himself while he watched her until she was completely out of view. He'd never felt quite so bad in his whole life.

Meg spent the rest of the week trying to practice her exercises and not think about Steve and Daphne. David didn't say much, but he spoke to Steve one evening just after she'd met him in the store, and Meg overheard enough to realize that Steve was taking Daphne out for the evening. It made her heart ache.

She telephoned the manager of her ballet company, Tolbert Morse, on Thursday.

"Glad you called," he said. "I think I may be on the way to meeting our bills. Can you be back in New York for rehearsals next week?"

She went rigid. In that length of time, only a miracle would mend her ankle. But she hesitated. She didn't want to admit the slow progress she was making. Deep inside she knew she'd never be able to dance that soon. She couldn't force the words out. Dance was all she had. Steve had made his rejection of Meg very blatant. Any hope in that area was gone forever.

Her dream of a school of ballet for little girls was slowly growing, but it would have to be opened in Wichita. Could she really bear having to see Steven all the time? His friendship with David would mean having him at the house constantly. No. She had to get her ankle well. She had to dance. It was the only escape she had now! Steven's latest cruelty only punctuated the fact that she had no place in his life anymore.

Fighting down panic, she forced herself to laugh. "Can I ever be ready in a week!" she exclaimed. "I'll be there with my toe shoes on!"

"Good girl! I'll tell Henrietta you'll want your old room back. Ankle doing okay?"

"Just fine," she lied.

"Then I'll see you next week."

He hung up. So did Meg. Then she stood looking down at the receiver for a long time before she could bring herself to move. One lie led to another, but how could she lie when she was up on toe shoes trying to interpret ballet?

She pushed the pessimistic thought out of her mind and went back to the practice bar. If she concentrated, there was every hope that she could accomplish what she had to.

David paused in the doorway to watch her Friday afternoon when he came home from work. He was frowning, and when she stopped to rest, she couldn't help but notice the concern in his eyes, quickly concealed.

"How's it going?" he asked.

She grinned at him, determined not to show her own misgivings. "Slow but steady," she told him.

He pursed his lips. "What does the physical therapist say?"

Her eyes became shuttered and she avoided looking directly at him. "Oh, that it will take time."

"You're supposed to start rehearsing in a month," he persisted. "Will you actually be ready by then?"

"It's in a week, actually," she said tautly, and told him about the telephone call. He protested violently. "David, for heaven's sake, I'll be fine!" she burst out, exasperated to hear her own fears coming from his lips.

He stuck his hands into his pockets with a long sigh. "Okay. I'll stop. Ahmed's going to be here at six."

"Yes, I remember. And you don't have to look so worried. I know that he invited Steve and Daphne, too."

His shoulders rose and fell heavily. He knew what was going on, but he couldn't tell Meg. She looked haunted and he felt terrible. "I'm sorry."

She forced down the memories of her last meeting with Steven, the painful things he'd said. "Why?" she asked with studied nonchalance. She dabbed at her face with the towel around her neck. "I don't mind."

"Right."

She lifted her eyes to his. "What if I did mind, David, what good would it do? I ran, four years ago," she said quietly. "I could have stayed here and faced him, faced her. I let myself be manipulated and I threw it all away, don't you understand? I never realized how much it would hurt him...." She turned, trying to control her tears. "Anyway, he's made his choice now, and I wish him well. I'm sure Daphne will do her best to make him happy. She's cared about him for a long time."

"She's cared about him, yes," he agreed. "But he doesn't love her. He never did. If he had, he'd have married her like a shot."

"Maybe so. But he might have changed his feelings toward her."

He gave her a wry glance. "If you could see the way he treats her at the office, you wouldn't believe that. It's strictly business. Not even a flirtatious glance between them."

"Yes, but you said that it all came to a head when she quit."

He grimaced. "So it did."

Her heart felt as heavy as lead. She turned away toward the staircase. "Anyway, I'm going back to New York soon."

"Sis," he said softly. She paused with her back to him. "Can I help?"

She shook her head. "But, thanks." She choked. "Thanks a lot, David."

"I thought you might get over him, in time."

She studied her hand on the banister. "I've tried, you know," she said a little unsteadily. She drew in a small breath. "I do have my dancing, David. It will compensate."

He watched her go up the staircase with a terrible certainty that ballet wouldn't compensate for a life without Steve. Her very posture was pained. Her ankle wasn't getting any better. She had to know it. But she must know, too, that Steve wasn't going to give in to whatever he felt for her; not when he'd been hurt so badly before. David shook his head and went upstairs to his own room to dress.

The limousine was prompt. Meg didn't have many dressy things, but once she'd bought a special dress for a banquet. She wore it this evening. It was a strappy black crepe cocktail dress with a full skirt and a laced-up bodice. David gave her an odd look when she came downstairs wearing it.

"Ahmed will faint," he remarked.

She laughed, touching the high coiffure that had taken half an hour to put up. Little blond wisps of hair trailed around her elegant long neck. "Not right away, I hope," she murmured. "It isn't really revealing," she added, to placate him. "It just looks like it. It was a big hit when I wore it in New York City."

"This isn't New York City, and Steven's going to go through the roof."

The sound of his name made her heart leap. Her eyes flickered. "Steven can do so with my blessing."

He gave up trying to reason with her. But he did persuade her to add a lacy black mantilla to the outfit by convincing her that Steven might take his rage out on David instead of Meg.

The limousine was very comfortable, but Meg had the oddest feeling that she was being watched. She glanced out the back window and not one but two cars were following along behind.

"Who's in that second car, I wonder?" she murmured.

"Don't ask." David chuckled. "Maybe it's the mob," he mused, leaning close and speaking in a rough accent.

"You're hopeless, David."

"You're related to me," he replied smugly. "So what does that make you?"

She threw up her hands and laid her head back against the seat.

It was an evening she wasn't looking forward to. All week, she'd dreaded this. But once Ahmed was gone, she wouldn't need to see Steve again socially. She could avoid him until she left to go back to New York. Meanwhile, if the sight of him with Daphne cut her heart out, there was nobody to know it except herself.

Six

────────

Steven's reaction to the black dress was almost the same as it had been to the red one she'd worn before, only worse. Meg remembered too late that the dress she'd had on the night she and Steven had parted had been black, too.

After a rather strained but delicious meal, Meg headed for the entrance lobby while the men paid the bill.

An uncomfortable-looking Daphne excused herself. Meg only nodded with forced politeness and stayed where she was. She had no intention of sharing even a huge ladies room with her rival. Unfortunately that left her unexpectedly alone with Steve, when Ahmed and David also excused themselves. Steve was fuming.

"Was that deliberate?" he asked Meg, nodding toward her dress.

She didn't pretend ignorance. She pulled the mantilla closer around her shoulders. "No," she replied after a pause. "Not at all."

He leaned against the wall and stared down at her, oblivious to the comings and goings of other patrons. The buzz of conversation was loud, but neither of them noticed.

"You wore black the night we argued," he said tautly. He caught her gaze and held it hungrily. "You let me undress you and touch you." His face hardened. "My God, you do enjoy torturing me, don't you, Meg?"

"I didn't do it on purpose," she said miserably. "Why do you always think the worst of me?"

"I'm conditioned to it, because I'm usually right," he said through his teeth. He dragged his eyes away, looking toward where the others had disappeared. "Damn them for deserting us!"

His violent anger was telling. She moved closer, unable to resist the power and strength of him. His cologne was the same he'd worn then. She got drunk on the scent as she looked up into silver eyes that began to glitter.

His eyes darkened as she approached, stopping her in her tracks. She hadn't realized quite what she was doing.

"Feeling adventurous?" he asked with a cold smile. "Don't risk it."

She clutched her purse. "I'm not risking anything. I was just getting out of the way of the crowd."

"Really?" He caught her hand in his and jerked. Under the cover of his jacket, he pressed the backs of her fingers deliberately against the hard muscle of his upper thigh, holding it there. "Look at me."

She panicked and pulled back, but he wouldn't let go. His strength was a little frightening. "Steven, please!" she whispered.

"There was a time when you couldn't wait to be alone with me," he said under his breath. "When your hands trembled after you fumbled my shirt open. Does dancing give you that incredible high, Meg?" he asked. "Does it make you sob with the need for a man's body to bury itself deep in yours?"

She moaned at the mental pictures he was producing, shocking herself. She dragged her hand away and all but ran to escape him, blindly finding her way to her brother. She found him in the hall, on his way back to where he left her.

"There you are," he said. "Ready to go, sis?"

"Where's Ahmed?" she asked, flustered and unable to hide it.

"He'll be right here."

As he spoke, Ahmed came through another door, looking for a moment as if he were someone Meg had never met. Another man was with him, a smaller and very nervous man with uplifted hands, who was grimacing as Ahmed spoke in a cutting soft tone to him in a language Meg couldn't translate.

The smaller man sounded placating. He made a gesture of subservience and abruptly departed as if his pants were on fire.

Ahmed muttered something under his breath, his black eyes cruel for an instant as he turned to the Americans. He saw the apprehension in Meg's face and the expression abruptly vanished. He was the man she knew again, smiling, charming, unruffled.

He strode to meet her, bending to kiss her knuckles. "Ah, my dancing girl. Are you ready to sample the theater?"

"Yes, indeed," she said, smiling back.

"I will have the driver bring the car around."

"I'll, uh, help you," David said nervously, with an incomprehensible glance over Meg's head at Steven.

"What's going on?" Meg asked curiously.

"A problem with the car," Steven said suavely, smiling down at Daphne as he linked her hand in his arm. "Shall we go, ladies?"

They were on the sidewalk, when the world shifted ten degrees and changed lives. As Steven left the women to follow Ahmed and David across the street to where the limousine had just pulled up, a car shot past them and sounds like firecrackers burst onto the silence of the night.

It seemed to happen in slow motion. The car sped away. Steve fell to the pavement. Ahmed quickly knelt beside him and motioned the others back toward the restaurant.

Daphne screamed. David caught her arm and rushed her toward the building yelling for Meg to follow. But Meg was made of sterner stuff and terror gave her strength she didn't know she had. She ran toward Steve, not away from him, deaf to the warnings, the curses Steve was raining on her as she reached him.

"Get back inside, you little fool!" he raged, his eyes furious. "Meg, for the love of God...!"

She didn't register the terror that mingled with anger in his face. "You've been hit," she sobbed. Her hands touched him, where blood came through his torn jacket sleeve. "Steven!"

"Oh, my God, get her out of here!" he groaned to Ahmed. "Get under cover, both of you! Run!"

But Ahmed wouldn't go and Meg clung. She wouldn't be moved. "No!" she whispered feverishly. "If they come back, they'll have to get both of us...!" she blurted out, shaking with fear for him.

Sirens drowned out any reply he might have made. His stunned eyes held hers while Ahmed got to his feet in one smooth movement, and his gaze searched the area around them. Satisfied that no other would-be assassins were lurking nearby, Ahmed murmured something to Steven and moved away toward two men—a dark one and a fair one—with drawn pistols who made a dive for him, through the crowd that was gathering just as the police and paramedics rushed forward. Meg's heart stopped, but Ahmed apparently knew the men and allowed himself to be surrounded by them and escorted to safety.

Meg sat on the pavement next to Steve, holding his hand, while the paramedics quickly checked his arm and bandaged what turned out to be only a flesh wound. Her white face and huge eyes told him things she never would have. His fingers entwined in hers and he watched her with fascination while stinging medicine and antiseptic was applied to the firm muscle of his upper arm.

"I'm all right," he told her softly, his tone reassuring, comforting, but full of wonder.

"I know." She was fighting tears, not very successfully.

"We'd better get him out of here," the officer in charge said grimly, staring around. "Don't spare the horses. We'll be right behind you with your friends," he told Steve. "Young lady, you can come with me," he added to Meg.

"No." She shook her head adamantly. "Where he goes, I go!"

The policeman smiled faintly and moved away.

"Don't get possessive, Miss Shannon," Steve remarked without smiling. "I don't belong to you."

Meg began to realize just how possessive she was acting and she felt embarrassed and a little guilty. "I'm sorry," she said, falteringly. "I forgot about Daphne..."

His face closed up completely. He averted his eyes. "You were upset. It's all right." He got to his feet a little unsteadily. "Go with the others," he told her. He turned when she hesitated, his eyes flashing. "Will you send Daphne here, please?"

"Of course," she said through numb lips. "Of course, I will."

So much for feeling protective. She'd given herself away and he didn't care. He didn't give a damn. He was still bearing grudges for old wounds. Why hadn't she known that?

NO RISK, NO OBLIGATION TO BUY ... NOW OR EVER!

CASINO JUBILEE
"Scratch'n Match" Game

Here's how to play:

1. Peel off label from front cover. Place it in space provided at right. With a coin, carefully scratch off the silver box. This makes you eligible to receive two or more free books, and possibly another gift, depending upon what is revealed beneath the scratch-off area.

2. Send back this card and you'll receive brand-new Silhouette Desire® novels. These books have a cover price of $2.99 each, but they are yours to keep absolutely free.

3. There's no catch. You're under no obligation to buy anything. We charge nothing – ZERO – for your first shipment. And you don't have to make any minimum number of purchases – not even one!

4. The fact is thousands of readers enjoy receiving books by mail from the Silhouette Reader Service™ months before they're available in stores. They like the convenience of home delivery and they love our discount prices!

5. We hope that after receiving your free books you'll want to remain a subscriber. But the choice is yours – to continue or cancel, anytime at all! So why not take us up on our invitation, with no risk of any kind. You'll be glad you did!

YOURS FREE!

This lovely Victorian pewter-finish miniature is perfect for displaying a treasured photograph – and it's yours absolutely free – when you accept our no-risk offer.

He started to speak, but she was already walking away, her carriage proud despite the faint limp. He wondered if his heart might burst at the feelings that exploded into it. He couldn't tell her what was going on; she'd be safer that way.

"Steven wants you to go with him," Meg told Daphne, refusing to meet her shocked eyes. "He's at the ambulance."

"But, shouldn't you...?" Daphne asked uncertainly.

Meg looked at her. "He asked for you," she said unsteadily. "Please go."

Daphne grimaced and went, but there was something new in her face, and it wasn't delight. She passed one of the two men who had guarded Ahmed, the blond one, and smiled at him rather secretively. He gave her a speaking glance before a terse comment from his tall, dark partner captured his attention.

Meg watched curiously until her brother interrupted her thoughts. "Are you all right?" David asked.

"Yes," she said slowly. She moved toward the Arab while his companions were momentarily diverted by policemen. "Ahmed, are you okay?" she asked the tall man gently. "In the confusion, I suppose I acted like an idiot."

"No. Only like a woman deeply in love," he said gently, and he smiled. "I am fine. I seem to invite Allah's protection, do I not? I have not a scratch. But I would not have had my friend Steven shot on my account."

"He'll be fine. Steve's like old leather," David said, chuckling with relief. "They're waiting for us."

"I don't suppose anyone would like to explain what's going on to me?" she asked the men when they were situated in the back of the police car heading toward the hospital.

David thought carefully before he replied. "We're selling some pretty sophisticated hardware to Ahmed's country. He has a hostile neighbor, a little less affluent, and they've made some veiled threats. We've had our security people and some government people keeping an eye on them. Tonight, they came out in the open with a bang. They're making their protests known in a pretty solid way."

"You mean they tried to kill Steve because you bought a plane?" she gasped, turning to Ahmed.

Ahmed grimaced. He exchanged a complicated glance with David and then shrugged. "Ah, that is so. Simplified, of course, but fairly accurate."

"They tried to kill Steven. Oh, my gosh!" she burst out.

"Equally simplified and fairly accurate," David added grimly. It wasn't the truth, but he couldn't tell her what was.

"Steve does have government protection?" she asked.

"Of a certainty." Ahmed gestured over his shoulder, and Meg saw a big black car following them and the police car ahead of them that carried Steven and Daphne.

"Who are they?" she asked nervously.

"CIA," David said. "They had us under surveillance, but nobody really expected this to happen. Now, of course, we'll be on video if we sneeze."

"You're kidding!" Her voice sounded high-pitched and uncertain.

There was a tiny noise and she jumped as "Gesundheit," came in an amused drawl from the police car's radio.

Steven was patched up, given a tetanus shot and released with an uneasy Daphne at his side. Ahmed and David kept Meg too busy talking to suffer too much at the sight.

Then they were all taken to police headquarters where two tall, tough-looking men—the same two who'd surrounded Ahmed after the shooting—sat down with the group and began to ask questions of everyone except Ahmed. That gentleman had been met by a small group of very respectful Arabs who surrounded him and preceded him into another room. It didn't occur to Meg just then to wonder why, if Steve was the target, these government agents had rushed to protect Ahmed.

As he spoke with his people, Ahmed, again, looked like someone considerably more important than a minor cabinet minister of a Middle Eastern nation. His very bearing changed when he was approached, and he seemed not only more elegant, but almost frighteningly implacable. The liquid black eyes, which for Meg had always been smiling, were now icy cold and threatening. He spoke to the men in short, succinct phrases, which the other Arabs received with grimaces and something oddly like fear.

Meg frowned at the byplay, drawn back into the conversation by the CIA.

"Are you a permanent resident of Wichita?" the blond one asked.

She shook her head. "No. I live and work in New York most of the time. I've had a small injury..."

"Left ankle, torn ligaments, physical therapy and rest for one more week," the big, dark-headed agent finished for her. Her mouth fell open and he leaned forward. "Gesundheit," he said, grinning wickedly.

David laughed. "Meg, I hope you don't have any skeletons in your closet."

Meg suddenly remembered the night in Steve's car and flushed. She didn't dare look at him, but the big, dark agent pursed his lips and deliberately turned his head away. She could have gone through the floor.

There were a few more questions and some instructions, but it was soon over and they were allowed to leave.

Ahmed was in the hall with the other Arabs. The government agents greeted him with quiet respect and a brief conversation ensued. He nodded, said something in Arabic to his companions and moved forward to say goodbye to his friends.

Meg came last. He took her hand in both of his, and the dark authority in his face made her start. This was not the charming, pleasant, lazily friendly man she thought she knew. Ahmed was quite suddenly something out of her experience.

"I hope that the evening has not been too strained for you, *mademoiselle*. I hope to see you again soon, and under kinder circumstances. *Au revoir*."

He kissed her hand, very lightly. With a nod to Steve and David, he strode back toward his men. They surrounded him quickly, flinging hurried, respectful questions after him, and followed him out into the night with the big dark government man a step behind.

Meg had the oddest feeling about Ahmed. She had to bite her tongue to keep the words from tumbling out. But her concern now was only for Steve. Her eyes slid around to where he was standing close to Daphne and the tall blond agent. "They'll catch the men who tried to kill him, won't they?" she asked David worriedly.

"Sure they will. Don't worry, now, it's nothing to do with you." He held up a restraining hand when she opened her mouth to ask some more questions. "Steve was barely scratched, despite the amount of bleeding. He'll be carefully looked after. Everything's fine."

"What is Steve selling to Ahmed?" she asked agitatedly.

"A fighter plane. Very advanced. All the latest technology. The government approves, because we're allies of Ahmed's strategically placed little nation."

"But if they're trying to stop the sale, why shoot at Steve?"

Meg was too quick. "Probably, they were shooting at both of them but Steve got the bullet," he said.

"Oh." She relaxed a little. "But what if they try again?"

"I told you, they're going to be surrounded by government people."

"Won't they try to get Ahmed out of the country now?"

David grimaced. "I don't know. Calm down now, Meg. Try not to worry so much. It's all under control, believe me."

Meg finally gave in. David did look less concerned now, and she had to accept that Steve would be protected from further attacks.

David, meanwhile, was shaking inside. What he and Steven had learned from the CIA agents and Ahmed was enough to terrify anyone. Ahmed couldn't go home just now, and while he was in Wichita, he was in mortal danger. It was far more serious than a protest over an arms sale. A coup was in progress in Ahmed's nation and Ahmed had been targeted by its leaders.

Ahmed's position was top secret, so Meg couldn't be told. Only Daphne knew, because of her engagement to Wayne Hicks, the blond CIA agent. She was an unofficial liaison between the government men and Ahmed. There were secrets within secrets here. It was a tricky situation, made more so by Steven's apparent relationship with Daphne while Meg stood by helplessly and fumed.

Meg glanced at Steven. "Are you going to be all right?" she asked without meeting his eyes.

"I'm indestructible," he said tautly. "I only needed a bandage, believe it or not. I'd better get Daphne home," he added.

"Thanks, Steve," Daphne said gently, smiling up at him.

Meg looked away, so she didn't see Daphne's expression or Steve's. Her heart was breaking. She smiled dully and took David's arm. "In that case, I'll take my brother and go home. Good night, then."

David got them a cab right outside the door. Presumably Daphne was going to drive Steven's Jaguar.

Meg sat quietly in the corner of the cab, still trying to focus on the shocking, violent events of the night. The shots, Steve's wound, Ahmed's incredible transformation from indulgent friendliness to menacing authority, the police, the government men, the hospital...it all merged into a frightening blur. Meg closed her eyes on the memories. Daphne had won and the only course of action Meg had was to concede the field to the other woman once more. If Steve loved her, she'd stay and fight. But he didn't. Hadn't he made it abundantly clear that he preferred Daphne?

Always before, she'd had the sanctuary of her New York apartment to run to. But now, with her ankle in this shape, she knew for certain that it would be a very long time before she was fit enough to dance again. A very, very long time. She had to consider a new career. If she couldn't dance, she had to find a way to support herself. A ballet school was the ideal way. She'd studied ballet all her life. She knew she could teach it. All she required was a small loan, a studio and the will to succeed.

The fly in the ointment was that it would have to be here in Wichita. New York City was full of ballet schools, and rental property cost a fortune. She'd never be able to afford to do it there. Here in Wichita, she was known in local circles, even if the family was no longer wealthy. Her roots went back four generations here. The downside was that she'd have to see Steven occasionally, but perhaps she could harden her heart.

Meanwhile, Steven and David would be fine now, surely, with the CIA watching. And of course, they'd get Ahmed out of the country.

But, would *she* be fine, she wondered? It was like losing Steven all over again. She didn't know how she could bear it.

Meg went to bed and didn't sleep. Steve had taken Daphne home. She was tormented by images of Daphne in Steven's arms, being thrilled and delighted by his kisses. She couldn't bear it.

She couldn't sleep on Friday night, and was listless all day Saturday and Sunday. She worked on her exercises, but her lack of progress just made her more depressed. She went to sleep on Sunday night, but again couldn't rest easily. She got out of bed and decided to go down for a cup of hot chocolate. Maybe it would help her sleep.

She opened her door and heard movement downstairs. Her first thought was that it might be a burglar, but the lights were all on.

She went to the banister and leaned over. David was in the hall putting on a raincoat.

"David?" she called, surprised.

He glanced up at her. He held a briefcase under his arm. "I thought you were asleep."

"I can't sleep."

"I know. Well, I've got to run this stuff over to Ahmed . . ."

"It's midnight!"

He glowered at her. "Ahmed doesn't recognize little things like the hour of the night. And before you start worrying, I've got an escort waiting outside. Try to get some sleep, will you?"

She sighed. "Okay. Be careful."

"Sure thing."

She wandered back into her bedroom. She heard a door slam twice and David's car pulling away. Odd, two slams, but she was sleepy. Perhaps she'd counted wrong.

She looked at herself in the mirror, in the sexy little lavender night slip that stopped at her upper thighs. She looked very alluring, she decided, with her hair down her back and those spaghetti straps threatening to loosen the low bodice that didn't quite cover the firm swell of her creamy breasts. She sighed.

"Too bad your hair's not platinum," she told her reflection. "And your legs are too long." She made a face at herself before she opened the bedroom door and wandered slowly downstairs, careful not to let her weak ankle make her fall as she negotiated her way down. A cup of hot chocolate might just do the trick.

She yawned as she ambled into the kitchen. But she stopped dead at the sight of the man standing there, staring at her with eyes that didn't quite believe what he was seeing.

"Steven!" she gasped.

He was fully dressed, a light blue sports jacket paired with navy slacks, a white shirt and a blue striped tie. But there was no bulge high up on his left arm, no bandage.

"Why are you here?" she asked bluntly, getting her breath back. She refused to try to cover herself. Let him look, she thought bitterly. "And do try to remember not to sneeze," she added, glancing around paranoidly. "They're probably got video cameras everywhere. Oh, Lord!" she added suddenly, glancing down at her state of undress and remembering that dark-haired agent with the wicked smile.

"There are no hidden cameras here," he returned. "Why would there be?" His silver eyes narrowed. "Which is just as well, because I don't want anyone else to see you like this."

"For your eyes only?" she taunted. "Well, save it all for Daphne, Steve, darling. What do you want here? David just left."

"I know. I'm here to keep an eye on you while he's gone." He shouldered away from the door facing. "You aren't planning to cut your visit short and go back to New York, are you?" he asked bluntly.

She didn't want to answer that. Her ankle was killing her this morning, from the slight exercise it had been put through the night before. She could hardly walk on it. The thought of dancing on it made her nauseous.

"Am I being asked to leave town?" she hedged.

"No. Quite the contrary." He stuck his hands into his pockets and studied her through narrowed eyes. "I think it might be better if you stay in Wichita. But don't go out without David, will you?"

"They shot at you, not me," she reminded him, and had to choke down the fear the words brought back. He could have been killed. She didn't dare think about it too much. "You're really all right, aren't you?" she added reluctantly.

"I'm really all right." He saw the concern she couldn't hide, but he knew better than to read too much into it. She'd loved him once, or thought she had, before she decided that dancing was of prime importance. He stared at her with growing need. Dressed that way, she aroused him almost beyond bearing. He didn't know if he could keep his hunger for her under control. That gown...!

She stared down at her bare feet. "I'm glad you weren't hurt."

He didn't reply. When she looked up again, it was to find his silver eyes riveted to her breasts, to the pink swell of them over her bodice. The look was intimate. Hungry. She could almost see his heartbeat increasing.

"Don't, Steve," she said quietly.

"If not me, who, then?" he asked roughly, moving slowly toward her. "You won't give yourself to anyone else. You're twenty-three and still a virgin."

She gnawed her lower lip. "I like it that way," she said unsteadily, because he was close now, towering over her. She could feel the heat of his body, smell the spicy cologne he wore. It was a fragrance that she'd always connected with him. It aroused her.

"The hell you do. You waited for me. You're still waiting." His silver eyes dropped to her bodice and found the evidence of her arousal. "You can't even hide it," he taunted huskily. "All I have to do is look at you, or stand close to you, and your body begins to swell with wanting me."

She swallowed. "Don't humiliate me!" she whispered tightly.

"That isn't what I have in mind. Not at all." His hands came out of his pockets. They moved slowly to the smooth curve of her shoulders and caressed away the tiny spaghetti straps. His breath was at her temple, on her nose, her mouth. She ached for him in every cell of her body.

"Steve." She choked. "Steve, what about Daphne ... ?"

"Daphne who?" he breathed, and his mouth settled on hers as his hands moved abruptly, sending the gown careening recklessly down her body to land in a silken lavender pool at her feet.

Seven

Right and wrong no longer existed separately in Steve's tormented mind. Meg wanted him and he wanted her. All the pain and anguish of the past four years fused in that one thought as he felt her mouth soften and open under his. He kissed her until she went limp in his arms, until his own body went rigid with insistent desire. And only then did he lift his head to look at what his hands had uncovered.

Meg felt the impact of Steven's eyes on her bare breasts like a hot caress on her skin. She stood before him in only a pair of lacy, high-cut pink briefs, insecure in her nudity. But when her hands lifted automatically, he caught her wrists and drew her hands to his chest. His steely eyes held hers while he pressed them there.

"Don't hide from me," he said quietly. His eyes fell to her body and sketched its pink and mauve contours with slow, exquisite appreciation. "You're more beautiful than a Boticelli nude, Mary Margaret."

"You're forgetting Daphne." She choked out the words, beyond protest. "She has a hold on you."

He was still staring at her, unblinking. "You might say that."

"Steve..."

"Don't talk, Meg," he replied, his voice deep and soft, almost lazy as his dark head started to bend toward her. "Talking doesn't accomplish a damned thing."

"Steven, you mustn't...!"

"Oh, but I must," he breathed as his mouth opened just above her taut nipple. "I must...!"

She felt the soft tracing of his tongue just before the faint suction that took her breast right into the dark warmth of his mouth.

Steve heard her gasp, felt her whole body go rigid in his grasp. But he didn't stop. He nuzzled her gently and increased the warm pressure. A little sound passed her lips and then she began to push toward him, not away from him. He groaned against her as his hands slid up the silky softness of her back and drew her into the aroused curve of his body.

Meg had stopped thinking altogether. The insistent hunger of his mouth made her body throb in the most incredible way. She cradled his dark head against her, leaning back in his embrace. She felt as if she were floating, drifting.

Steve was kneeling, easing her down to the floor, his mouth against her. He pulled her over him, parting her smooth legs so that they were hip to hip. His mouth moved to her other breast, then to her throat and finally up to her parted lips. He kissed her with slow, aching passion, all the while exploring her body with deft, sure hands. He whispered things she couldn't even hear for the roar in her ears. And then he shifted her, just a little, and she felt the aroused thrust of him as his body began to rock sensually against hers.

She gasped and stiffened, because even their most intimate time hadn't been quite this intimate.

He lifted his head. His silver eyes were misty with desire as he searched hers. He moved, deliberately, so that she felt him intimately, and a wave of pleasure rippled up her body. She couldn't hide the shocked delight in her eyes. He smiled, slowly, and moved again. This time her hands gripped his shoulders and she relaxed, shyly bringing him into even greater intimacy with her.

His lean hand slid up her thigh, tracing its inner curve. She saw his mouth just before it settled on hers again. He touched her as he never had. Waves of pleasure jolted her. She tried to protest, but it was far too late. She began to whimper.

His tongue tangled with hers, thrust deep into her mouth. She felt tears in her eyes as he held her in thrall. Her body arched helplessly toward him. She felt his mouth sliding down to her breasts, possessing her. He stroked her until she was weeping with helpless desire, her voice breaking as she whispered, pleaded, begged.

The husky pleas, combined with the sensual movement of her body over his, removed him sufficiently
from reality so that it was impossible for him to pull
back in time. He kissed her. His mouth bit into hers
and she felt him move, felt the soft tearing of her
briefs, felt the air on her body. She heard the rasp of
a zipper, the metallic sound of a belt.

He pulled her up so that she was sitting with her legs
on either side of him. She heard his breathing, rough
and unsteady at her ear, as his lean hands suddenly
gripped her bare thighs deliberately and he lifted her.

"Easy," he whispered as he brought her to him and
slowly pulled her down.

She had a second to wonder about the faint threat
of his hold on her, and then his mouth opened on hers
and she felt the first insistent thrust of him against the
veil of her innocence.

Her eyes flew open. She cried out at the flash of hot
pain. He held her still, breathing roughly. His face was
rigid, his teeth clenched, his breathing audible through
his nose. He looked into her wide, frightened eyes and
held them as he pulled her slowly down on him again.

"Don't be afraid, Meg," he whispered deeply. "It's
only going to hurt for a few seconds."

"But...Steve..." She gasped, trying to find the
words to protest what was happening.

"Let me love you," he said unsteadily. His hands
tugged her over him and he shivered. His face was
tormented, his eyes like silver fires. "God, baby...let
me. Let me!" He ground out the words.

She knew that it would be impossible for him to
stop. She loved him. That was all that really mattered

now. She gave in, yielding to the pain, her hands taut on his shoulders. Her hold on him tightened and she flinched.

"Just a ... little further. Oh, Meg," he growled, shivering as he completed the motion and felt her all around him. His eyes closed and he shivered. Then they opened again and searched hers as he repeated the slow, deliberate movement of his hips until his possession of her was complete and the lines of strain left her face. Then he rested, his body intimately joined to hers, and gently pushed her disheveled hair back from her face.

She swallowed. There was awe in her eyes now, along with lingering pain and doubt and shock.

"I've waited so long, Meg," he said unsteadily. "I've waited all my life for this. For you."

Her fingers trembled on his shirtfront. "Steve, you're ... part of me," she burst out.

Color burned along his high cheekbones. "Yes." He moved, as if to emphasize it, and she blushed. "Unfasten my shirt, Meg. Let me feel your breasts against my skin while we love."

While we love. She must be insane, she thought. But she was too involved to stop, to pull back. She was in thrall to him. Her hands fumbled with his tie, his jacket, his shirt. She fumbled, but finally she stripped it all off him.

Her hands speared through the thick mat of hair that covered him from collarbone to below his lean waist. She looked down and stared helplessly, her body trembling. His powerful hands lifted her up just a little, smiling even through his need at the expression on her face.

"Steve..."

He tilted her face and brought his mouth down on her lips with exquisite tenderness as he began to guide her hips again. This time there was no pain at all. There was a faint pleasure that began to grow, to swell, to encompass her. She gasped and her nails bit into his shoulders.

"Like this?" he whispered, and moved again.

She sobbed into his shoulder, her mouth open against his neck, clinging to him as he increased the rhythm and pressure of his body. His hand clenched in the hair at her nape and he caught his breath, shivering.

"Relax, now," he said, sliding a hand under her thigh to pull her to him roughly. "Yes...!"

His image began to blur in her open, startled eyes as the pleasure became suddenly violent, insistent. She felt herself tense as he lifted to her as they knelt so intimately together, shivering with every movement, reaching for something she couldn't quite grasp. Her strength gave out, but his was unfailing, endless.

"Help me," she whispered brokenly.

"Tell me how it feels, Meg," he whispered back, his voice rough, deep as he pushed up insistently. "Tell me!"

"It's so sweet...I can't...bear...it!" She wept.

"Neither can I." His hands tightened on her thighs almost to bruising pain and he lost control. "Meg.... Meg....!"

She felt him go rigid just before her mind was submerged in a heated rush of pleasure. It was a kind of pain, she thought blindly. A kind of sweet, unbearable pain that hit her like a lightning bolt, lifting her in his arms, making her cry out with the anguish it kindled. She didn't know if she could bear it and stay alive.

Steven's heart was beating. She felt the heavy, hard beat against her breasts, felt the blood pulsating through him as he eased her down on her back, still a part of him. He relaxed, his arms catching the bulk of his weight while he struggled to breathe normally. The intimacy of their position was beyond her wildest dreams. She closed her eyes, experiencing it through every cell of her body.

He could hardly believe what he'd done. The rush of pleasure had almost knocked him out. He'd been so desperate for her that he hadn't even removed all his clothing. He'd fought them both out of their garments and taken her sitting up on the carpet, when her first time should have been in a bed with their wedding night before them and everything legal and neatly tied up. And worst of all, he hadn't had the foresight to use any sort of protection. He groaned aloud as sanity came back in a cold rush. "Oh, hell!" He ground out the words.

He levered himself away from her and got to his feet a little shakily. He zipped his trousers with a vicious motion of his hands before he fumbled a cigarette out of the pocket of his discarded shirt and lit it. He put on his shirt. He didn't look at Meg, who finally managed with trembling hands to slide her gown back on. The briefs were beyond wearing at all.

Steve smoked half the cigarette before he crushed it out in an ashtray on the table, one that David kept for him. He buttoned his shirt and replaced his tie and jacket before he spoke.

By then, Meg was sitting on the very edge of the sofa, feeling uncomfortable and very ashamed.

He stood over her, searching for the right words. Impossible, really. There weren't any for what he'd done.

"You'll be sore for a while," he said stiffly. "I'm sorry I couldn't spare you the pain."

She wrapped her arms around herself and shivered.

He knelt just in front of her, his hand on the sofa beside her as he searched her wan, drawn face.

"Meg," he said roughly, "it's all right. You don't have anything to be ashamed of."

"Don't I?" Tears rolled down her cheeks.

"Oh, baby," he groaned. He pulled her down into his arms and sat on the carpet, cradling her against him. His lips found her throat and pressed there gently. "Meg, don't cry."

"I'm easy, I'm cheap . . . !"

"You are not." He lifted his head and held her eyes. "We made love to each other. Is that so terrible? If I hadn't gone crazy and chased you away, it would have happened four years ago, and you know it!"

She couldn't really argue with that. He was telling the truth. "Will you tell Daphne?" she asked.

"No, I won't tell Daphne," he replied quietly. "It's none of her business. It's no one's, except ours."

She still felt miserable, but some of the pain eased away as he smoothed her against him. Her eyes closed and she wished that she never had to move away again. He was warm and strong and it felt right to be lying with him this way. What had happened felt right.

His lean hand smoothed over her flat belly. He drew back a little and stared down at it, his face troubled.

She knew what he was thinking. It had just occurred to her, too.

"You didn't use anything," she whispered.

"I know. Damn me for a fool, I was too far gone to care." He lifted his eyes to hers and grimaced. "I'm sorry. It was irresponsible. Unforgivable."

Her blue eyes sketched his dark face, down to his stubborn chin and the breadth of his shoulders.

"What are you thinking?" he asked curiously.

"You were an only child," she said. "Did your father have any sisters?"

He shook his head. His brows curved together and then a smile tugged at his firm mouth as he searched her eyes. "Boys run in my family, Meg. Is that what you wanted to know?"

She nodded, smiling shyly.

His big hand pressed slowly against her belly. "A baby would cost you your career," he said slowly.

She looked up at him. "You don't think my ankle won't?"

The expression drained out of his face, leaving it blank. "What do you mean?"

She threw caution to the wind. It was time for honesty. Total honesty, despite the cost. She'd truly burned all her bridges.

"It hurts just from walking. It's swollen. It's been weeks, and it's no better." She traced a pearly button on his shirt with her fingernail as she forced herself to face the fear she'd been avoiding. "Rehearsals begin at the end of next week, but it might as well be yesterday. Steve, I won't be able to dance. Not for a long time. Maybe not ever."

He didn't move. His eyes searched her face, but he didn't speak, either.

She looked up at him miserably. "What will happen to you and Daphne if I get pregnant? It would ruin everything for you." She sighed wearily, closing her eyes as she laid her cheek on his chest. "Oh, Steve, why is life so complicated?"

"It isn't, usually."

"It is right now." She bit her lower lip. "Would you...want a baby?"

His body began to throb. Light burst inside him. A child. A little boy, perhaps, since they ran in his family. A bond with Meg that nothing could break. The thought delighted him.

But he didn't answer immediately, and Meg thought the worst. She had to fight tears. "I see," she said brokenly. "I guess you'd want me to go to a clinic and—"

"No!"

"You wouldn't?"

"Of course I wouldn't!" he said curtly. He held her face up to his. "Don't you even think about it! I swear to God, Meg, if you do anything...!"

"But, I wouldn't!" she said quickly. "That's what I was going to tell you. I couldn't!"

He relaxed. His hand moved to her cheek and brushed back the disheveled hair around its flushed contours. "Okay. Make sure you don't. People who don't want babies should think before they make them."

"Like we just did," she agreed with a flicker of her dry humor.

He lifted an eyebrow. "Right."

She relaxed a little more. He did look marginally less rigid and austere. "I could have said something."

"Of course. Exactly when did you think of saying something?"

She flushed and dropped her eyes.

"That's when I thought of saying something. It was a bit late, of course." He frowned slightly and his silver eyes twinkled. "It was very intense, wasn't it? Even for you."

"I'd wanted you for a long time," she confessed quietly.

"And I, you." He drew in a long, slow breath. "Well, it's done. Now we have to live with it. I'll get your ring out of the safe and bring it over. We are now officially reengaged."

"But Steve, what about Daphne?" she exclaimed.

"If you mention Daphne one more time today, I'll—!" he muttered. He let her go and got to his feet, pulling her up beside him. "She'll understand."

"You haven't asked if I want to be engaged again," she protested, trying to keep some control over her own destiny.

He pulled her to him and his hand curved around her flat stomach. "If you've got a baby in here, you don't have much choice. My mother would bring the shotgun all the way from West Palm Beach and point it at both of us before she'd see her first grandchild born out of wedlock.''

She smiled, picturing his mother staggering under the weight of one of Steven's hunting rifles. ''I guess she would at that.'' She glanced at him wryly. ''And I'd already be sitting on your doorstep wearing a sign —*and* maternity clothes—so that everyone would know who got me pregnant in the first place.''

He felt the world spin around him. He mustn't read too much into that beaming smile on her face, he told himself. After all, with her ankle in this condition, she had no career left. He was still second best in her life. At least she would want a child, if they'd made one.

She looked up and encountered the cold anger in his face and knew instantly that despite his hunger for her, all the bitterness was still there.

He shrugged. Bending, he pushed back her tousled hair. ''I want you. You want me. Whatever else there is, we'll have that.'' He sighed gently. ''Besides, if the attraction we feel is still strong enough four years after the fact to send us making love on the carpet, it isn't likely to weaken, is it?''

''For heaven's sake, Steve!'' she exclaimed, outraged.

''Meg, you're repressed.'' He shook his head. ''What am I going to do with you?''

''You might stop embarrassing me,'' she muttered.

His eyebrow jerked as he stared at her. ''My beautiful Mary Margaret,'' he said softly. ''When I wake up in the morning, I'll be sure that I was only dreaming again."

"Did you dream of me?" she asked involuntarily.

"Oh, yes. For most of my life, I think." He searched her soft eyes. "'There be none of Beauty's daughters with a magic like thee...'" he quoted tenderly, and watched the heat rise in her cheeks. "Do you like Lord Byron, Meg?"

"You never read poetry to me," she said with a sad little smile.

"I wanted to. But you were very young," he recalled, his face going hard. "And I was afraid to trust my heart too far." He laughed suddenly as all the bitterness came sweeping back. "Good thing I didn't. You walked out on me."

"You made me," she shot right back. "You know you did." The anger eased as she saw the pained look on his face. "You haven't had a lot of love, Steven," she said. "I don't think you trusted anyone enough to let them close to you—not Daphne, and certainly not me. You like my body, but you don't want my heart."

He was shocked. He stared at her, searching for words. He couldn't even manage an answer.

"I'd love you, if you'd let me," she said gently, her blue eyes smiling at him.

His jaw clenched. "You already did, on the floor," he said coldly. All sorts of impossible things were forming in his mind. He felt vulnerable and he didn't like it. He glared at her. "You didn't even try to stop me. Since you can't dance anymore, what a hell of a meal ticket I'll make!"

She stared at him and suddenly saw right through the angry words. She knew with a flash of intuition that he was still fighting her. He cared. Perhaps he didn't know it. Perhaps he'd even convinced himself that he really loved Daphne. But he didn't. Even though she was innocent, Meg knew that men didn't lose control as Steve had tonight unless there were some powerful emotions underlying the desire. He was fighting her. It had been that all along, his need to keep emotional entanglements at bay. He was afraid to risk his heart on her. Why hadn't she seen that years ago?

"No comeback?" he taunted furiously.

She smiled again, feeling faintly mischievous. "Are you going to bring my ring back tonight?"

He hesitated. "Meg..."

"I know. It's way after midnight and David will be home soon, I suppose," she added. "But you could come to supper tomorrow night. And bring my ring back," she emphasized. "I hope you haven't lost it."

He glared at her. "No, I haven't lost it. I can't bring it tomorrow night. I have a dinner meeting with Ahmed. Daphne's coming along," he reminded her.

She felt a little uncertain of her ground, but something kept her going, prodded her on.

She moved toward him, watching his expressions change, watching his eyes glitter. She caught him by the lapels and went on tiptoe, softly brushing her body against his as she reached up and drew her mouth tantalizingly over his parted lips. She could feel his heartbeat slamming at his ribs, hear his breathing. He was acting. It was a sham. She bit his lower lip, gently, and let go of him, moving away.

"What was that all about?" he asked gruffly.

"Didn't you like it?" she asked softly.

His jaw clenched. "I have to go."

"To dinner, perhaps. But not to Daphne's bed. Not now."

"What makes you so sure that I won't?" he demanded with a mocking smile.

She searched his eyes. "Because it would be sacrilege to do with anyone else what we just did with each other."

He would have denied it. He wanted to. But he couldn't force the words out. He turned and went to the door, pausing just to make sure the lock was on before he glanced back.

"Buy a wedding gown," he said curtly. "And if you try to run away from me this time, I'll follow you straight to hell if I have to!"

He closed the door behind him, and Meg stared at it with a jumble of emotions, the foremost of which was utter joy.

Steve was feeling less than pleased. He had Meg, but it was a hollow victory. Despite the exquisite pleasure she'd given him, he was no closer to capturing her heart. He wanted it more than he'd ever realized.

She cared about him. She must, to give herself so generously. For Meg, physical need alone would never have caused such a sacrifice. But he had to remember that her career was no longer a point of contention between them. Her career was history. Even if she cared about him, ballet would have come first if it had been an option. He knew it. And that was what made him so bitter.

Eight

Later that same night, after a refreshing shower, Meg went to bed, feeling tired. But she barely slept at all, wondering at the way things had changed in her life.

David gave her curious looks at the breakfast table. "You look like you haven't slept at all," he remarked.

"I haven't," she confessed, smiling at him. "Steven and I got engaged again last night."

He caught his breath. The delight in his eyes said everything. "So he finally gave in."

"Not noticeably," she murmured dryly.

"He's taken the first step," he replied. "You can't expect a fine fighting fish to just swallow a hook, you know."

"This fighting fish is a piranha. He's very bitter, David," she said quietly. She sipped coffee, her brows knitted. "He's never really forgiven me for leaving—even though he drove me away."

He smiled at her, his eyes kind and full of warmth. "I gather that he'll be over tonight?"

"Probably not. I doubt if Daphne can spare him," she muttered. "He's having dinner with her."

He grimaced at the expression on her face. He knew what was going on, and that Steve couldn't tell her. Neither could he.

"Things aren't always what they seem," he began.

"It doesn't matter, you know," she replied with resignation. "I love him. I never stopped. The past four years have been so empty, David. I'm tired of running from it. At least he still wants me, you know. I may not win entirely, but I'll give Daphne a run for her money," she added with a tiny smile.

"That's the spirit. You might consider, too, that if he didn't care, why would he want to marry you?"

She couldn't tell him that. She changed the subject and led him on a discussion of local politics.

But she did go around in a daze for the rest of the day. She wouldn't have believed what had happened if it hadn't been for the potent evidence of it in her untried body. Her memories were sweet. She couldn't even be bothered to worry about Daphne anymore. She did worry about Steven. If a crazed terrorist was after him, how would the authorities be able to stop him? And what about Ahmed?

The questions worried her, so she found solace in her exercises. Even so, she only did them halfheartedly. Ballet had been her life for years, but now she thought about loving Steven and having a baby of her own. Suddenly her fear of childbirth seemed to diminish, and her disappointment over her injury faded. Ballet was a hobby. It was nothing more than a hobby. She was daydreaming now, of little baby clothes and bassinets and toys scattered around a room that contained Steven and herself as well as a miniature version of one of them. Anything seemed possible; life was sweet.

Steven tossed and turned until dawn and went into the office in a cold, red-eyed daze. His life had shifted without warning. He'd made love to Meg and nothing would ever be the same again. If he was besotted with her before, it was nothing to what he was now that he'd known her intimately. He wasn't certain that he could even work.

Daphne brought in the mail. She saw his worried expression and paused in front of the desk.

"Something's wrong, isn't it?" she asked with the ease of friendship. "Can I help?"

"Sure," he agreed, leaning back in his big desk chair. "Tell me how to explain to Meg, to whom I've just become reengaged, why I'm going out with you tonight."

She whistled. "That's a good one."

"Isn't it?"

"Can't you get permission to tell her the truth?"

He shook his head. "Your own fiancé told me not to tell. He thinks too many people are in the know already." He closed his eyes with a long sigh. His body was pleasantly tired and still faintly throbbing from its exquisite knowledge of Meg.

"Isn't she going back to New York temporarily?" Daphne asked.

"I'm afraid to let her," he said wearily. "At least here she can be protected along with David. But I can't tell her what's going on. I'm going to have to ask her to trust me, when I never trusted her."

"If she loves you enough, she will," Daphne said with certainty. "And anyway, surely it will all be over soon."

"God, I hope so!"

"How's the arm?"

"Is wasn't exactly a major wound," he mused, chuckling. "The bullet broke a small vein. I've got a bandage over it. Funny, I didn't even notice—" He broke off, feeling uncomfortable as he remembered the night before, when he and Meg had both forgotten it. He changed the subject, quickly. "Have we heard from Ahmed today?"

She grimaced. "Indeed we have. He came in surrounded by bodyguards and government agents, and eventually chewed up one of the girls in the typing pool, who stopped bawling long enough to take a leaf out of my very own book. She threw a paperweight at him on his way out."

"What?"

"Calm down, it was a very small paperweight—not in the same league as the lamp I threw at you—and she missed on purpose, too," Daphne said quickly, with a grin. "He was surprised, to say the least. In his country, women don't react like that."

"I don't guess they do. Certainly not with Ahmed!"

"But, then, Brianna our typist didn't know who he was," Daphne reminded him. "And she still doesn't. She told me that if he sets foot in the building again, she's quitting," she added. "She is a very angry young lady, indeed."

"I need to have a word with your fiancé," Steve said. "Just to see what else needs doing so we can wind up this mess."

"Ahmed's under twenty-four-hour guard. He's used to it, of course. I understand he had a slight altercation with his bodyguard when they didn't see the assassins coming last night."

"I noticed the bruises," Steven mentioned.

"I'm sorry about Meg," Daphne said, grimacing. "I seem to keep complicating things for her."

"Not your fault this time," he said. "Or last time, either. It was my pride that sent her running. I hope I'll have better luck now."

"So do I," Daphne told him sincerely. "We're good friends, Steve. We always have been. I'm so happy. I hope you're going to be, too, you and Meg."

He only nodded. "We'd better get to work."

"Yes, sir," she said with a grin. "I'll send Wayne in."

Daphne's fiancé was blond and blue-eyed, a screaming contrast to his partner, who was tall and very dark and had a sense of humor that had already sent Steven up the wall.

The dark one looked around very carefully, even peering under Steve's desk.

"Looking for bugs?" Steve asked with a twinkle in his eyes.

"No," he replied. "Paperweights and blue-eyed brunettes." He grinned. "She's a dish."

"Yes, she is, but you're on duty," Wayne told his partner.

"So I am." He straightened, wiped the smile off his face and stared grimly at Steven. "Sir, have you noticed any bombs or enemy missiles in your office—oof!"

Wayne calmly removed his elbow from his friend's ribs. "I'm going to feed you to a shark on our next assignment."

The taller man lifted both bushy eyebrows. "Copycat. James Bond did that to an enemy agent in one of his films."

"Are you sure you're suited to this line of work, Lang?" Wayne asked somberly.

"Plenty of people with badges have a sense of humor." Lang glared at his friend. "Plenty more don't, of course."

"To the matter at hand," Wayne interrupted, glancing at Steve. "We need your itinerary for the rest of the week, right down to the minute. And if you plan any more impromptu evening outings..."

"Not me," Steven said with a slow grin, indicating his arm. "I've gone right off night life without adequate protection."

"Fair enough. We're now in the process of bugging everything you own, from cars to houses to aircraft, as well as Mr. Shannon's home," Wayne continued, noticing Steve's faint color with absent curiosity. "We would have done it sooner, but until this morning we hadn't quite decided about how much surveillance was required. It would be pretty stupid to overlook protection for your chief executive, Mr. Shannon, and his sister, especially since they were seen in the company of Ahmed. These people will use whatever bargaining tools they can get, and Ahmed's fondness for Miss Shannon was pretty obvious.''

Steve didn't like remembering that. He was jealous of Ahmed now—jealous of any man who looked at Meg.

''Isn't it dangerous politically to let Ahmed stay here, in the States?'' Steve asked suddenly.

''Certainly,'' Lang told him. ''Suicidal, in fact.'' He grinned and his dark eyes twinkled. ''But we're responsible for him. So if we send him home and somebody blows him away, guess who gets the blame?''

''We're in between a rock and a hard place,'' Wayne agreed. ''That's why we're going to keep Ahmed here and see if we can draw the other agents out into the open again.''

''They were in the open last night.''

''Ah,'' Lang replied, ''but it was just a routine surveillance until then. We didn't have any advanced warning of an assassination try until the coup attempt was made in Ahmed's home country. And by then the terrorists were already in position here and making their move. Now that we know what's afoot, we're ready, too.''

''We're on it. We'll handle this. How about Miss Shannon?'' Wayne asked Steven. ''Can you get her out of town?''

"I can," Steven agreed. "But what if they find out that she and I are engaged again and make a grab for her, where she's totally unprotected?"

The smile vanished from Lang's face. "You're engaged again?"

Steven nodded.

Lang exchanged a long glance with Wayne. "That changes things. We'd better keep her in town. But she can't know why," he emphasized.

Steven just nodded, because Wayne had already told him that. He could break their confidence, of course, but now that the house and his car and God knew what else was bugged, he couldn't tell Meg anyplace that they wouldn't overhear. He was going to have to watch what he said altogether. And the complication was that he not only couldn't tell Meg that, but he wouldn't be able to touch her without being overheard. He could have groaned out loud.

Meg was home alone that afternoon. David was still at work.

Steven drove up to the Shannon house just a few minutes after quitting time, casually dressed in jeans and a knit shirt, topped off with a suede jacket.

He smiled at Meg when she opened the door, approving the pretty blue sundress that complemented her fairness. She'd left her hair down, and he ached to get his hands in its silky length.

"Give me your hand," he said without preamble.

She lifted the left one, and he slid the sapphire and diamond engagement ring he'd given her four years ago smoothly on to her ring finger. It was a perfect fit.

He lifted the hand to his lips and kissed it very gently.

"Oh, Steve," she whispered, reaching up to him.

He caught her wrists and stepped back, painfully aware of surveillance techniques that could pick up heavy breathing a mile away. He laughed a little shortly, trying to ignore Meg's shocked, embarrassed expression.

"How about some coffee?" he asked.

She faltered a little. "Of course," she said. "I'll, uh, I'll just make some." She was near tears. They'd made love, they'd just gotten reengaged, and suddenly Steven couldn't bear her to touch him!

He followed her into the kitchen, grimacing at her expression. He couldn't tell her everything, but he had to tell her this, at least.

As she turned on the faucet to fill the drip coffee maker, Steve reached over her shoulder and took the coffeepot away, leaving the water running just briefly.

He bent to kiss her, whispering under his breath, "We're on Candid Camera."

She let him kiss her, but her wide eyes stayed open. He drew back, shutting off the faucet.

She was suddenly very alert. She looked around the room. "Achoo?" she whispered.

"Gesundheit!" came the deep, chuckled reply.

Meg went every shade of scarlet under the sun as she looked at Steven. She gasped in horror.

"It's all right," he said quickly. "They've only just done it!"

She chewed the ends of her fingers as the flat statement finally began to make sense and she relaxed. "Oh, thank goodness!"

The back door opened and the big, dark agent entered, a finger to his lips.

He whipped out a pad and pencil and wrote something on it, showing it to Meg and Steve. He'd written: *Our team wasn't the only one wrangling bugs around here this afternoon. Watch what you say.*

Do they have cameras? Steve scribbled on the paper.

The agent shook his head, grinning. He made a sign with two forked fingers like someone poking eyes out.

Steve gave him a thumbs-up sign. The agent put away his pad and pencil and looked at the coffeepot longingly.

Meg held up five fingers. He grinned and started back out. Then he glanced at the two of them and made a kissing motion followed by a firm shaking of his head. Meg stuck her tongue out at him. He smothered a laugh as he let himself back out the door.

Meg busied herself with the coffeepot, worried about living in a goldfish bowl. It would be like this from now on, she was sure, until they caught the people who were responsible for the attack at the restaurant.

"Cream?" Steven asked when she poured coffee into two cups.

"I'll get it."

She handed it to him, carrying a cup of black coffee to the back door. A huge hand came out and accepted it. She peered around the door, eyebrows raised. The agent made a sign with his thumb and forefinger and eased back around the side of the house with his cup.

Meg closed the door gently and followed Steve back into the living room.

"I can't stay long. I have a date," he told Meg.

She glared at him. "Of course. With Daphne."

"And Ahmed," he replied. "At the Sheraton. More business discussions."

It didn't occur to her right then why Steve had given away his movements, when he knew the house was bugged. "I don't suppose I could come along?" she asked.

"No."

"I like Ahmed. He likes me, too."

"Of course he likes you. You're blond."

She glared at him.

"And pretty."

The glare softened.

"And very, very sweet."

She smiled.

He sipped his coffee. "Where are we going to live when we're married?"

"I like Alaska . . ."

He glowered at her. "In Wichita, Meg. I don't work in Alaska."

"What's wrong with your house?" she asked.

"It doesn't have much of a yard," he replied. "We'll need a place for a swing set and some outdoor playthings for the kids."

She flushed, averting her eyes. "So we will."

He stared at her until she lifted her face, and he smiled. He slid his arm over the back of the couch and his eyes narrowed. His head made a coaxing motion.

She put her coffee cup down, her blood throbbing in her veins, and went across to join him on the sofa.

He put his thumb over her mouth and pulled her down into his arms. As his hand lifted, his lips parted on her mouth, and he kissed her with long, slow passion. His hand found her breast, teasing the nipple to hardness while he kissed her as if he could never get enough.

When he lifted his head, her eyes were misty and dazed, her body draped over his lap.

He looked at her for a long, long time.

"I have to go," he said quietly.

She started to protest, but she knew that it would do no good at all.

"Will I see you tomorrow?" she asked miserably as he helped her up.

"Probably." He stood close to her, his eyes troubled. "Lock the doors. David will be home soon."

"My brother is a poor substitute for my fiancé," she muttered.

"It won't always be like this," he said solemnly. His silver eyes searched hers for a long time. "I promise you it won't."

She nodded. "Do be careful. The way you drive..." She stopped when he frowned. "Well, I'd like to think you could get all the way home in one piece."

He lifted an eyebrow. "Do you worry about me?"

"All the time," she said honestly, her blue eyes wide and soft.

His heart raced as he looked down at her. If she was putting on an act, it was a good one.

Gently he brought her against him and bent to brush his open mouth softly over her own. She moved closer. His arms enfolded her, cherished her. She wrapped herself around him and gave way to the need to be held.

But things got out of hand almost immediately. He caught her hips and pushed her away, his face set in deep, harsh lines as he fought to control his passion for her.

"Go back inside," he said huskily. "I'll phone you in the morning."

"Why did you bother to get engaged to me when you plan to spend your nights with another woman?" she asked miserably.

"You know why," he said, his voice deep, his eyes glittering. "Don't you?"

Because they'd stepped over the line and she might be pregnant. How could she have forgotten? She moved back from him, averting her eyes.

"Yes," she replied, freezing up. She'd tried to forget, but he wasn't going to let her. She was weaving daydreams. The reality was that he'd lost his head and now he was going to do the honorable thing. "Of course I know why, Steven. Silly of me to forget, wasn't it?"

He scowled and his face tautened. She had the wrong end of the stick again. But he couldn't, didn't dare, say anything. "David should be here any minute," he added. "Don't go outside, and lock the door after me."

"I'll do that."

He glanced around. Nothing and nobody was in sight, but he was certain that one of the agents guarding Meg was nearby. He'd arranged that before he left the office.

"I'll phone you tomorrow. Maybe we can go out."

"What a thrill," she said.

He glared at her. "Keep it up."

"I'm trying."

He made an exasperated sound, stuck his hands into his pockets and moved toward his Jaguar.

After he drove away, Meg closed the door and locked it, and went back into the living room.

David came home long enough to change and went right back out again, apologizing to Meg. He had to go along with Steve and Daphne to hobnob with Ahmed.

"Is everybody going except me?" Meg groaned, exasperated.

David grinned at her. "Probably. Have a nice evening, now."

She glared at him. He left and she busied herself watering her house plants. The house was unusually quiet, and she kept imagining noises. They made her uneasy, especially under the circumstances. She heard movement in the living room and slowly stuck her head around the door to see what it was, her heart pounding madly.

But it was only the big dark agent standing there, grinning at her. He put a finger to his lips, pushed a button on some small electronic device in his hand, and chuckled as it emitted a jarring noise.

"There'll be plenty of headaches tonight," he murmured dryly.

"What did you do?" she asked, and then clapped a hand over her mouth.

"It's okay. I jammed them." He studied her through narrowed eyes. "I need to talk to you."

"What about?" she asked, and waited almost without breathing for the answer.

He was serious then, the twinkle gone from his dark eyes. He towered over her, almost as tall as Steve and just about as intimidating. He pushed the button on the jamming device with a calculating look on his face, shutting off the interference.

"I'm going to get you out of here, right now. Tonight. I want you to come with me, no arguments."

She hesitated. "Shouldn't we call Steve or your partner?"

"No one is to know. Not even my partner."

She didn't like the sound of that. She liked this man, but she didn't completely trust him.

"Why isn't your partner to know?" she asked curiously.

He muttered something under his breath. Then he calmly pulled out his automatic pistol and leveled it at her stomach. He seemed to raise his voice a little. "Because he would try to stop me, of course," he replied. "I plan to turn you over to Ahmed's buddies outside. You'll be a hell of a bargaining tool for them."

"You can't do this!" she exclaimed, thinking of ways to escape, but unable to come up with anything. There was an automatic pistol pointed at her stomach. She'd heard it said that even a karate black belt would hesitate to fight off an armed man.

"But I can," he assured her. "In fact, I'm doing it. Let's go."

Nine

Meg felt her breath catch in her chest as she stared down numbly at the muzzle of the pistol. Dozens of wild thoughts passed through her mind, none of which lingered long enough to register except one: she was never going to see Steve again.

Her blue eyes lifted to Lang's dark ones. He didn't look as if he meant to kill her.

He jerked his head toward the front door and indicated that he wanted her to go out it. "I said let's go," he said. "Now."

She hesitated. "Can't we . . . ?"

He took her arm firmly and propelled her forward. She felt the presence of the gun, even if she didn't feel it stuck in her back. She noticed that he looked around from side to side as if he was expecting company.

Perhaps the enemy agents would shoot him. But that wasn't likely. If they'd overheard what he said, and that jammer had seemed to be turned off at the last, they'd be waiting out here for him to turn her over to them. Would they pay him? Of course they would. They'd keep her hostage and use her to trade to Steve for Ahmed. She felt sick.

"Hey!" he called as they got to the front porch. "Let's make a deal, boys. I'm cutting myself in on the action!"

"You turncoat," Meg cried furiously.

"Stop struggling," he said calmly. "How about it!"

"We have already heard you," came a distinctly accented reply. "How much do you want for the woman?"

Lang turned toward the voice. "Let me come over there and we'll talk about it. No shooting."

"Very well!"

A shadowy figure appeared. Lang measured the distance from where the car was to where the man was and began to walk down the middle of it with Meg.

"Keep your nerve," he said unexpectedly. "For God's sake, don't go to pieces now."

"I'm not the screaming type," she muttered. "But I am not going to let you give me to those people without a fight!"

"Good. Uh, don't start fighting until I tell you, okay? I breathe better without extra holes in my chest." He lifted his head and marched her quickly forward, beginning to veer almost imperceptibly when the car was in running distance.

"Wait! Stop there!" the voice called.

Lang broke into a run, dragging Meg with him. The sudden movement startled the two men who were in view now. Guns were raised and Lang groaned.

"Stop!" the accented voice warned harshly. "Do not attempt to enter the car!"

Lang stopped at his dark blue car with the hand holding the pistol on the door handle and lifted his head. The wind whipped his dark hair around his face. "Why not?" he called back. "It's a great night for a ride!"

"What are you doing?!"

"I thought it was obvious," he replied. "I'm leaving."

"You agreed to bargain! Let the girl go and you may go free!"

"Make me."

He pushed Meg into his car and locked the door from the passenger side. He jumped in on the other side and started the car. After a glance in the rearview mirror, he dropped it in gear, and shot off as two men came into view. Shots were fired into the air, but he didn't even slow down.

Meg felt sick. She huddled against her door, wondering frantically if it would kill her to force the handle and jump out at the speed they were going. Lang's actions were more puzzling by the minute. Was he holding out for a better price?

"Don't be a fool," Lang said curtly. He didn't look at her, but he obviously knew what she was considering. "You'd be killed by inches."

"Why?" She groaned. "Why?"

"You'll find out. Be a good girl and sit still. You won't come to any harm. I promise."

"Steve will kill you," she said icily.

His eyebrow jerked. "Probably," he murmured. "He'll have to wait in line. It was all I could think of on the spur-of-the-moment." He glanced in the rear-view mirror and mumbled something about a force the size of NATO coming up behind, in a jumble of international agents.

"They're chasing you?" She smiled gleefully. "I hope they shoot your tires out and kidnap you and sell you into slavery!"

He chuckled with pure delight, glancing at her. "Are you sure you want to be engaged to Ryker? I'm two years younger than he is and I've got an aunt who'd pamper you like a baby."

"She'll be very ashamed of you when you end up in prison, you traitor!" she accused.

He shook his head. "Oh, well. Duck, honey."

"Wha...?"

He pushed her down and dodged as a bullet came careening through the windshield, leaving shattered glass all over the front seat, including Meg's lap.

"Oh, my God!" she screamed.

"Keep your head," he said curtly. "Don't panic."

Another bullet whizzed past. She kept her head down, mentally consigning him to the nether reaches.

"Exciting, isn't it?" he shouted above the gunfire and the roar of the engine. His dark eyes glittered as he weaved along the highway just ahead of his pursuers. "God, I love being a secret agent!"

She stared at him from her hiding place on the floorboard as if he were a madman.

He was singing the theme song from an old spy TV show, zigzagging the car on the deserted highway as more bullets whizzed past.

"Hold on, now, here we go!"

He hit the wheel hard. Tires spun on the pavement, squealing like banshees, and they were suddenly going in the opposite direction across the median. Blue lights flashed and sirens sounded.

"The police!" she gasped. "Oh, boy! I hope they fill you full of lead! I hope they mount your head on a shortwave antenna and throw the rest of you to the buzzards! I hope...!"

He grabbed for the mike on his two-way radio. "Did you get the signal? Here they are, boys. Go get 'em!" he said into it.

He stopped the car and as Meg peered over the broken dash, three assorted colors and divisions of police car went flying across the median and after the horrified occupants of the two cars that had been in hot pursuit of Meg and Lang.

"Now, admit it," he said, breathing heavily as he turned to her, grinning. "Wasn't this more exciting than watching some stupid game show on TV? The thrills, the chills, the excitement!"

She felt sick all over. She started to speak and suddenly wrenched the door handle. He pushed the unlock button on the driver's armrest just in the nick of time. Meg lost everything she'd eaten earlier in the day.

* * *

Lang passed her a handkerchief and managed to look slightly repentant when she was leaning back against the seat of the police car that had picked them up when one carful of enemy agents was in custody.

"They ought to put you in solitary and throw away the key," the young police lieutenant told Lang when Meg had finished sipping the thermos cup of strong black coffee he'd fetched for her. "You poor kid," he told Meg.

"I told you, it was all I could think of," Land replied, lounging nonchalantly against the rear fender of the police car. "I overheard them talking. They were going to snatch her. So I jammed their signal into the house to get their attention, then let them hear me selling her down the river. I beeped you guys once we were in the car to let you know something was going down. I didn't have time to do any more than that. They were headed toward the house when I decided to get her out."

"You didn't have to hold a gun on her!" the policeman raged.

"Sure I did," he replied. "She's a fighter. She was going to argue or maybe start a brawl with me. But when I pointed the pistol at her, she went with me without a single argument. And because they thought I was going to hand her over to them, they didn't shoot at me until it was too late."

"I still say..."

With a long suffering sigh, Lang pulled out his automatic and slapped it into the policeman's palm.

The officer stared at him, puzzled.

"Well, look at it," Lang muttered.

The policeman turned it over and sighed, shaking his head.

Lang held his hand out. When the weapon was returned to it, he pulled the missing clip out of his pocket, slammed it into the handle slot and cocked it, before putting on the safety. Then he slid it back into his underarm holster and snapped it in place.

"It wasn't loaded?" Meg asked, aghast.

"That's right," Lang told her. He glowered at her. "And you thought I was selling you out. She called me everything but a worm," he told the policeman. "A traitor, a turncoat. She said she hoped they hung my head on a radio antenna!"

The policeman was trying not to laugh.

"I didn't know you were trying to protect me," Meg said self-consciously.

"Next time, I'll let them have you," he said irately. "They can throw you into somebody's harem and I hope they dress you in see-through plastic wrap!"

The policeman couldn't hold it back any longer. He left, quickly, chuckling helplessly.

"I like that," Meg said haughtily. "At least I'd look better in it than you would!"

"I have legs that make women swoon," he informed her. "*Playgirl* begs me for photo sessions."

"With or without your gun?" she countered.

He grinned. "Jealous because you don't have one? Pistol envy?"

She burst out laughing. Lang was incorrigible. "All right, I apologize for thinking you sold me out," she told him. "But you were pretty convincing. I had no idea you had on a mask, figuratively speaking."

"You'd be amazed at how much company I have," he said dryly. He glanced up as a car approached. "Oh, boy."

She looked where he was staring. It was a big black limousine. Her heart leaped when it stopped and a white-faced, shaken Steven jumped out, making a beeline toward Meg.

He didn't break stride except to throw a heated punch at Lang, which the younger man deflected.

"She's okay," Lang said, moving back. "I'll explain when you cool off."

"You'd better do your explaining from someplace where I can't reach you," Steve replied, and he looked murderous.

"I told you!" Wayne raged, moving into view behind Steve. "You idiot, I told you not to do things on your own!"

"If I hadn't they'd have carried her off!" Lang shot back, exasperated. "What was I supposed to do, call for reinforcements from the trunk of their damned car on the way to the river?"

"They wouldn't throw you in any river, you'd pollute it and kill the fish!"

Lang's voice became heated as the two men moved out of earshot. Steven paused just in front of Meg and looked down at her from a strained face.

"Are you all right?" he asked tersely.

"Yes, thanks to Lang," she replied. "Although I wasn't exactly thanking him at the time," she added, nodding toward the remains of the car Lang had rescued her in.

Steve didn't look at it very long. It made him sick. He reached for Meg and pulled her hungrily into his arms. He held her bruisingly close, rocking her, while his mind ran rampant over all the horrific possibilities that had kept him raging all the way to the scene after Wayne had gotten the news from the city police about the chase.

"I guess your evening with Daphne was spoiled?" she asked a little unsteadily.

"If anything had happened to you, I don't know what I'd have done," he groaned.

She eased her arms under his jacket and around him, holding on. It was so sweet to stand close to him this way while around them blue and red lights still flashed and voices murmured in the distance.

"You'd better get her home, sir," the police officer said gently. "Everything's all right, now."

"I'll do that. Thanks."

He led her back to the limousine. "What about Lang?" she asked Steve. "And didn't his friend... Wayne... ride with you?"

"They can go with the police or hitchhike," Steve said. "Especially Lang!"

"What about Daphne...?"

"I'm taking you home, Meg," he said. "Nobody else matters right now."

"Is David there?"

He nodded. "He doesn't know about any of this. I didn't want to worry him."

She crawled into his lap when the chauffeur started the car, to Steve's amazement.

"Your seat belt," he began.

"I've had my close call for tonight," she told his chest. "Let me stay."

His arms curved around her, pulling her closer. They rode home like that, without a word, cradled together.

David turned white when he learned what had happened. "But how did they know?" he groaned.

"The house is bugged," Meg said, sitting down heavily on the couch. "Lang had some sort of jamming device . . ."

"He blew up the bugs," David explained. "Scrambled their circuits. One of the agents explained that device to me, but I hadn't seen one until I got home. When I saw it lying here, and you were gone, I knew something had happened. But I couldn't find out anything."

"Sorry," Steven said. "I took off out the door the minute I heard what had happened, with Wayne two steps behind me. I didn't want to worry you." He grimaced. "I have to phone Daphne and tell her where we are."

Meg didn't look at him as he lifted the receiver on the telephone and dialed.

"I'll go up and change my things," she told David. She had pieces of glass on her skirt and in her hair. "It's been a pretty rough night."

"I can imagine. You're limping!"

"I always limp," she said dully. "It's worse because I've walked on it." She laughed mirthlessly. "I don't think it's going to get any better, David. Not ever."

He watched her go with quiet concern. Steve hung up the phone after he'd explained things to Daphne and turned to David.

"This whole thing is getting out of hand," he said tersely. "I can't take much more of it. She looks like a ghost, and that damned fool agent could have killed her driving like that!"

"What if he hadn't gotten her out of the house, Steve?" David asked, trying to reason with his friend. "What then?"

It didn't bear thinking about. Steve stuck his hands into his pockets. "My God."

"How about some coffee?" David asked. "I was about to make a pot."

"I could drink one. They'll have Ahmed under guard like Fort Knox by now. I'll go up and see about Meg. She was sick."

"That doesn't surprise me. Her ankle is bothering her, too." He turned to Steve. "She's not going to be able to dance. You know that, don't you?"

Steve nodded. "Yes, I know it. Why else do you think she's willing to marry me?" he added cynically. "We both know that if she really had a choice, her damned career would win hands down."

"Try to remember that neither your father nor our mother wanted Meg to marry you."

"I know that."

"And Meg was very young. Afraid, too." He studied Steve. "Has she explained why?"

Steve looked hunted. "She gave me some song and dance about being afraid of pregnancy."

"She wasn't afraid of it, she was terrified. Steve," he added quietly, "she was with our sister when she died in childbirth. She was visiting during that snowstorm that locked them in. She watched it happen and couldn't do a thing to help."

Steven turned around, his face contorted. "Meg was there? She never said anything about that!"

"She won't talk about it still. It affected her badly. All this happened while you were away at college. Meg was only ten years old. It was, is, a painful subject. It was never discussed."

"I see." Poor Meg. No wonder she'd been afraid. He hadn't known, her father had told him, but at the time he had not felt comfortable asking questions. He felt guilty. He wondered if she was still that afraid, and hiding it.

"Go on up and get Meg. I'll fix that coffee," David said, clapping his friend on the shoulder.

Meg was just climbing out of the shower when Steve opened the bathroom door and walked in.

She gasped, clutching the towel to her.

"You blush nicely," he mused, smiling gently. "But I know what you look like, Meg. We made love."

"I know, but..."

He took the towel from her hands and looked down at her, his silver eyes kindling with delight. "Pretty little thing," he mused. "I could get drunk on you."

"David is just downstairs," she reminded him, grabbing at her towel. "And spies have bugged the whole house. They're probably watching us right now!"

"They wouldn't bug the bathroom," he murmured dryly.

"Oh, wouldn't they?"

He moved toward her, pulling her into his arms. "No," he whispered, bending. "Is this better? I'll hide you, Meg, from any eyes except my own."

She felt his mouth nibble softly at her lips, teasing them into parting.

"You taste of mint," he whispered.

"Spearmint toothpaste," she managed to say.

"Open your mouth," he whispered back. "I like to touch it, inside."

She shivered a little, but she obeyed him. His hands smoothed over her firm breasts, savoring their silky warmth as he toyed with her mouth until she felt her body go taut with desire.

"I want you," he breathed into her mouth. His hands lifted her hips and pressed them to his. "We could lie down on the carpet in here and make love."

She felt his lips move down her throat until his mouth hungrily kissed her breasts.

"David—" she choked "—is downstairs."

"And we're engaged," he whispered. "It's all right if we make love. Even some of the Puritans did when they were engaged."

"Steve," she moaned.

He kissed her slowly, hungrily, moving his mouth over hers until she was mindless with pleasure.

"On second thought," he said unsteadily, lifting her gently into his arms, "the carpet really won't do this time, Meg. I want you on cool, clean sheets."

She looked up into his eyes, her arms linked around his neck. Her blond hair was pinned up. Wisps of it teased her flushed cheeks. His gaze went all over her, lingering on her breasts.

"You want me, don't you?" he asked, his voice deep and soft in the stillness of the room.

"I never stopped," she replied unsteadily. "But, Daphne...!"

"I don't sleep with Daphne," he said as his mouth eased down on hers.

Maybe that was why he wanted Meg, she thought miserably. But none of it made sense, much less his hunger for her. He lost control when he touched her, and she was powerless to stop him.

"Steve, I can't," she groaned as he leaned over her with dark intent.

"Why not?"

"David's just downstairs!" she exclaimed.

He was trying to remember that. But looking at Meg's beautiful nude body made it really difficult. She shamed the most prized sculptures in the world.

"Why did you never tell me that you were with your sister when she died?" he asked softly.

She stiffened. Her face drew up and the memories were there, in her wide, hurt eyes.

He smiled wryly and pulled the cover over her. He sat down beside her, fighting to control his passion. She'd had enough excitement for one night and she was right. This wasn't the time.

"Didn't you think I'd understand?" he persisted.

"You wanted me very much," she began slowly. "But you were so distant from me emotionally, Steve. The one time we came close to being intimate, you acted as if precautions didn't matter at all. And I was young, and shy of you, and very embarrassed about things like sex. I couldn't find the right way to tell you, so I froze up instead. And you blew up and told me to get out of your life."

"I'd waited a month to touch you like that," he reminded her. "I went overboard, I know. But you obsessed me." He smiled with self-contempt. "You still do, haven't you noticed? I touch you and I lose control. That hasn't changed."

"You don't like losing control."

He shook his head. "Not even with you, little one."

She reached up and touched his chin, his mouth. "I lose control when you touch me," she reminded him.

"You can afford to now. Your dancing won't come between us anymore."

"Don't sound like that. Don't be so cynical, Steve," she pleaded, her wide eyes searching his. "You're coming up with all sorts of reasons why I want to marry you, but none of them has anything to do with the real one."

"And what is the real one? My money? My body?" he added with a cold smile.

"You can't believe that I might really care about you, can you?" she asked sadly. "It's too much emotion."

"The only emotion that interests me is the emotion I feel when I've got you under me."

She colored. "That's sex."

"That's what we've got," he agreed. "That's all we've got, when you remove all the frills and excuses. And it will probably be enough, Meg. You can find a way to fill your time here in Wichita and spend my money, and I'll come home every night panting to get into bed with you. What else do we need?"

He sounded so bitter. She didn't know how to reach him. He was avoiding the issue because he couldn't find a way to face it.

"You said you wanted a child," she reminded him.

"I meant it." He frowned slightly, remembering what David had told him. "Did you mean it, Meg?"

"Oh, yes," she said gently. She smiled. "I like children."

"I've never had much to do with them," he confessed. "But I suppose people learn to be parents." He slowly pulled the cover away from her body and looked down at her with curious, quiet eyes. "I didn't think about anything that first time. Certainly not about making you pregnant." He touched her stomach hesitantly, tracing a pattern on it while she lay breathlessly looking up at him. "Meg, how would it be if we made love," he said slowly, meeting her eyes, "and we both thought about making a baby together while we did it?"

She felt her heartbeat racing. She stared at him with vulnerable eyes, her feelings so apparent that she could see his heartbeat increase.

"That would be...very exciting," she whispered huskily. "Wouldn't it?"

He drew her hand slowly to his body and let her feel the sudden, violent effect of the words. His breath stilled in his throat.

"Damn your brother," he said unsteadily. "I want to strip off my clothes and pull you under me, right here, right now!"

She reached up, tugging his face down. He kissed her with slow anguish, a rough moan echoing into her mouth. His hand explored her, touched and tested her body until he made it tremble. She whimpered and he clenched his teeth while he tried to fight it.

"We can't." She wept.

"I know. Oh, God, I know!" He brought her up to him and held her roughly, crushing her against him so that the silky fabric of his suit made a faint abrasion against her softness. "Meg, I need you so!"

"I need you, too," she murmured, shaken by the violence of her hunger for him. "So much!"

"Do you want to risk it?" he whispered at her ear. "It would have to be quick, Meg. No long loving, no tenderness." Then he groaned and cursed under his breath as he realized what he was offering her. "No!" he said violently. "Oh, God, no, not like that. Not ever again!"

He forced himself to let go of her. His grip on her arms was bruising as he lifted away from her and then suddenly let her go and turned away. He was shaking, Meg saw, astonished.

"I'm going to get out of here and let you dress," he said with his back to her. "I'm sorry, Meg." He turned around, slowly, and looked down at her. "I want lovemaking," he said quietly, "not raw sex. And we need to think about this. If you're not already pregnant, we need to think very carefully about making you that way.''

She smiled gently. He sounded different. He even looked different. "I don't need to think about it," she said softly. "But if you do, you can have all the time in the world.''

Color ran along his cheekbones. He looked at her with eyes that made a meal of her. Finally he closed them, shivering, and turned away from her.

"I'll see you downstairs," he said in a faintly choked tone. He went out without looking back and closed the door firmly.

Meg saw something in his face before he left the room. It was enough to erase every terror the night had held and give her the first real hope she'd had of a happy future with him.

Ten

But if Meg had expected that look in Steve's eyes to change anything, she was mistaken. He'd had time to get himself together again, and he was distant while he drank coffee with Meg and David downstairs. She walked him to the door when he insisted scant minutes later that he had to leave. David discreetly took the coffee things into the kitchen, to give them a little privacy.

"When this is over," he told Meg, "you're going to marry me, as quickly as I can arrange a ceremony."

"All right, Steven," she replied.

He toyed with a strand of her blond hair, not meeting her eyes. "Daphne isn't who you think," he said. "I can't say more than that. But a lot of people aren't what you think they are." He lifted his eyes to hers. "I'll tell you all of it, as soon as I can."

It was an erasing of doubts and fears. A masquerade, and almost time to whip off the masks. She searched his silver eyes quietly. "I care for you very much," she said simply. "I'm tired of fighting it, Steven. I'll be happy with what you can give me."

His jaw clenched. "I don't deserve that."

She smiled impishly. "Probably not, but it's true, just the same." She moved closer and reached up to kiss him very tenderly. "I'm sorry David wouldn't go away so that we could make love," she whispered. "Because I want to, very, very much."

"So do I, little one," he said tautly. "It gets harder and harder to stay away from you."

"But not hard enough to make you give up Daphne?" she probed delicately, and watched him close up.

"Give it time."

She shrugged. "What else can I do?" she asked miserably. She sighed and leaned closer, so that his mouth was against her forehead. "I love you," she said.

He held her with mixed emotions. She didn't quite trust him, but he hoped she was telling the truth about her feelings. He was in too deep to back out now. "I'll see you tomorrow. Lang had better be on his way to the moon," he added irritably.

"Don't hurt him," she said softly. "He really did save me."

"I know what he did," he muttered, and it was in his eyes when he lifted his head. "Maybe they'll give him to Ahmed as a going-away gift."

"Ahmed isn't going away, is he? I thought he was based in Washington, D.C."

Steve started to speak, but decided against telling her what he'd been about to say. "You'll understand everything in a day or two. Just a few loose ends to wrap up, now that Lang's precipitated things. Don't worry. You're all right now."

"Whenever I'm with you, I'm all right."

"Are you?" he asked dryly. "I wonder."

She drew back and smiled up at him. "Good night, Steven."

He stuck his hands into his pockets with a long sigh. "Under different circumstances, it would have been a hell of a night," he remarked. He studied her long and hard. "You're lovely, Meg, and much more than just physically pretty. I don't know why I ever let you go."

"You didn't feel safe with me. You still don't, do you?"

"You were a career ballerina," he reminded her.

"I was an idiot," she replied. "I didn't know you at all, Steven. I was young and silly and I never looked below the surface to see what things and people really were. You were afraid of involvement. Maybe I was, too. I ran for safety."

"You weren't the only one." His eyes narrowed. "But I get homicidal when you're threatened," he said quietly. "And you get hysterical when I am," he added. "Don't you think it's a little late for either of us to worry about getting involved now?"

She smiled ruefully. "We're involved already."

"To the back teeth," he agreed. He drew in a long breath. "In more ways than one," he added with a quick glance at her belly.

She laughed. "I was so afraid of it four years ago," she said softly. "And now, I go to bed and dream about it."

His hands clenched in his pockets. He searched her eyes closely. "It would really mean the loss of any hope of a career, even if your ankle heals finally," he said. "How could you take a child with you to New York while you rehearse and dance? How could you hope to raise it by long distance?"

"I thought I might teach ballet, here in Wichita," she began slowly. "It's something I know very well, and there are two other retired ballerinas in town who worked with me when I was younger. I could get a loan from the bank and find a vacant studio."

Lights blazed in his eyes. "Meg!" he groaned softly. He bent and kissed her, his mouth slow and tender.

She was stunned. Why, he didn't mind! When he drew back, the radiance in his face stopped her heart.

"I could help you look for a studio," he said, his voice deep and hesitant. "As for the financing, I could stake you at a lower interest than you could get from the bank. The rest of it would be your project."

"Oh, Steven!"

He began to smile. He lifted her by the waist and held her close. "Wouldn't you pine for the Broadway stage?"

"Not if I can work at something I love and still live with you," she said simply. "I never dreamed you'd accept it."

His eyes blazed into hers. "Didn't you?"

Her arms looped around his neck and she put her mouth softly over his, kissing him with growing hunger.

He tried to draw back and her arms contracted.

"Kiss me," she whispered huskily, and opened her mouth.

He made a sound that echoed in the quiet hall and she felt his tongue probing quickly, deeply, into the darkest reaches of her mouth while her body throbbed with sudden passion.

There was a ringing sound somewhere in the background that Steve and Meg were much too involved to hear.

A minute later there was a discreet cough behind them. Steve drew back and looked blindly over Meg's shoulder, his mouth swollen, his tall body faintly tremulous.

"That was Lang," David said with barely contained amusement. "He said to tell you that there's a surveillance camera in the hall and the other agents are discussing film rights."

Steve dropped Meg to her feet. He glared around at the ceiling. "Damn you, Lang!"

Meg leaned against Steve, laughing. "He's incorrigible. One day we'll hear that someone has suspended him over a pond of piranhas at the end of a burning rope."

"Please, give them some more ideas," Steve pleaded, glancing up again.

"Do you really think there are any they haven't already entertained? They're highly trained after all, right, Lang?" Meg called with a wicked grin.

Steve muttered something, dropped a quick kiss on Meg's lips and left the house.

The office was buzzing with excitement the next morning, all about the wild chase and the capture of enemy agents. Daphne had told half the people in the building, apparently, because Steve got wry grins everywhere he went.

Ahmed came in late in the morning, surrounded by his bodyguards. He looked a little pale and drawn, but he was smiling, at least.

Daphne started to say something to him, abruptly thought better of it and left him in Steve's office. The door closed softly behind her.

"Meg is all right?" Ahmed asked quietly.

"She's fine. And none the wiser for it," Steve replied heavily. He leaned back in his desk chair and propped his immaculate black boots up on the desk. "But I'm going to have a lot to say to Lang's superiors about the way he protected her. With any luck, they'll send him to Alaska to bug polar bears."

Ahmed smiled slowly. "I understand there was something of a stir among the surveillance people last evening. Something about man-eating fish and burning hemp..."

"Never mind," Steve said quickly. "What's the latest about the coup in your country?"

Ahmed sat down in the leather chair across from the desk and crossed one elegant leg over the other. His bearing was regal, like the tilt of his proud head and the arrogant sparkle in his black eyes.

"Ah, my friend, that is a story indeed," he said pleasantly. "To shorten it somewhat, the assassins captured last night by your government's agents were the weak link in a chain. We will learn much from them." Ahmed looked very hard when his eyes met Steve's.

Steve felt chills go down his spine. Ahmed had been his friend for a long time, but there were depths to the man that made him uneasy. He might not be a Moslem, but Ahmed was every inch an Arab. His thirst for vengeance knew no bounds when it was aroused.

"When do you leave for home?"

Ahmed spread his hands. "Today, if it can be arranged. The sooner the better, you understand." His black eyes narrowed. "I would not willingly have put you and Meg and David at risk. I hope you know this, and understand that it was not my doing."

"Of course I do."

"Meg...you have not told her?" he added carefully.

"I thought it best not to," Steve said. "The less she knows the safer she is. For now, at least."

Ahmed smiled. "I agree. She is unique, our Meg. If she did not belong to you, my friend, I could lose my heart very easily to that one."

"You're invited to the wedding," Steve replied.

"You honor me, and I would enjoy the occasion. But the risk of returning to your country so soon after this unfortunate attempt at an overthrow is too great.''

"I understand.''

"I wish you well, Steve. Thank you for all that you have done for my people—and for myself. I look forward to future projects such as this one. With your help, my country will move into the twentieth century and lessen the chance of invasion from outside forces.''

"Watch your back, will you?'' Steve asked. "Even with the culprits in custody, you can't be too careful.''

"I realize this.'' Ahmed got to his feet, resplendent in his gray business suit. He smiled at Steve as they shook hands. "Take care of yourself, as well, and give my best to your brother and the so beautiful Meg.''

"She'll be sorry that she didn't have the opportunity to say goodbye to you,'' Steve told him.

"We will meet again, my friend,'' he said with certainty.

Steven walked him to the outer office, where a slender, dark-haired girl was glaring at the Arab from behind a propped-up shorthand tablet with information that she was copying into the computer. She quickly averted her eyes.

Daphne motioned to Steve and pointed at the telephone.

"I'll have to go. Have a safe trip. I'll be in touch when we get a little further along in the assembly.''

"Yes.''

Steve shook hands again and went back into his office to take the telephone call.

Daphne hesitated, hoping to provide a buffer between the angry look in Ahmed's eyes and the intent look in Brianna's, but Steve hung up the telephone and buzzed her. She grimaced as she finally went to see what he wanted.

Ahmed stood over the young woman, his liquid black eyes narrowed as he glared at her. "You have had too little discipline," he said flatly. "You have no breeding and no manners and you also have the disposition of a harpy eagle."

She glared back at him. "Weren't you just leaving, sir?" she asked pointedly.

"Indeed I was. It will be pleasant to get back to my own country where women know their place!"

She got out of her chair and walked around the desk. Her pretty figure was draped in a silky dark blue suit and white blouse that emphasized her creamy complexion and huge blue eyes. She got down on her knees and began to salaam him, to the howling amusement of the other women in the typing pool.

"How dare you!" Ahmed demanded scathingly.

Brianna looked up at him with limpid eyes. "But, sir, isn't this the kind of subservience you demand from your countrywomen?" she asked pleasantly. "I would hate to offend you any more than I already have. Oh, look at that, a nasty bug has landed on your perfectly polished shoe! Allow me to save you, sir!"

She grabbed a heavy magazine from the rack beside her desk and slammed it down on his shoe with all her might.

He raged in Arabic and two other unintelligible languages, his face ruddy with bad temper, his eyes snapping with it.

Daphne came running. "Brianna, no!" she cried hoarsely.

Ahmed was all but vibrating. He didn't back down an inch. Daphne motioned furiously behind her until Brianna finally got the hint and took off, making a dash for the ladies' rest room.

"In my country..." he began, his finger pointing toward Brianna's retreating figure.

"Yes, I know, but she's insignificant," Daphne reminded him. "A mere fly speck in the fabric of your life. Honestly she is."

"She behaves like a savage!" he raged.

Daphne bit her tongue almost through. She smiled tightly. "You'll miss your flight."

He breathed deliberately until some of the high color left his cheekbones, until he was able to unclench the taut fists at his side. He looked down at Daphne angrily. "She will be punished." It was a statement, not a question.

"Oh, yes, of course, she will," Daphne swore, with her fingers tightly crossed behind her back. "You can count on that, sir."

Ahmed began to relax a little. He pursed his lips. "A month in solitary confinement. Bread and water only. Yes. That would take some of the spirit out of her." His dark eyes narrowed thoughtfully. "It would be a tragedy, however, to break such a beautiful wild spirit. Do you not think so?"

"Indeed," Daphne agreed quickly.

He nodded, as if savoring the thought. "Your country has such odd people in it, *mademoiselle*," he said absently. "Secret agents with quirks, secretaries with uncontrollable tempers . . ."

"It's a very interesting country."

He shrugged. "Puzzling," he corrected. He glanced at her. "This one," he nodded toward the door where Brianna had gone. "She is married?"

"No," Daphne said. "She has a young brother in a coma. He's in a nursing home. She has no family."

His dark brows drew together. "No one at all?"

She shook her head. "Just Tad," she replied.

"How old is this . . . Tad?"

"Ten," Daphne said sadly. "There was an automobile accident, you see. Their parents were killed and Tad was terribly injured. They don't think he'll ever recover, but Brianna goes every day to sit by his bed and talk to him. She won't give up on him."

His face changed. "A woman of compassion and loyalty and spirit. A pearl of great price indeed."

Daphne heard the buzzer and went to answer it, leaving Ahmed to rejoin Steve.

Steve put the Arab on a plane—a chartered plane owned by Ahmed's government—later that morning, with Daphne and two taciturn American agents at his side.

"Have a safe trip," Steve said.

"How can I help it?" Ahmed muttered, glancing at the number of armed guards in his country's uniform gathered at the walkway to the plane. "Many thanks for your help," he added to the agents, and Daphne, who was standing close to the tall blond agent.

"It was our pleasure. Anytime," Wayne replied.

Lang grinned at him. "Just give us a day's notice and we'll cover you like tar paper, sir," he replied.

Steve glared at him. "And watch your every move on hidden cameras," he added icily.

"What can I tell you?" Lang sighed, lifting his hands and letting them fall. "I *am* a spy, after all. I get paid to spy on people. It's what I do." He looked somber as he faced Ahmed. "You'd just be amazed at the things you see on a hidden camera, sir. Like last night, for instance..."

Steve moved toward him threateningly.

Lang grinned. "Actually," he clarified, "I meant this rich guy we were watching who likes to play video games and when he wins, he takes off all his clothes and pours Jell-O over himself."

"So help me!" Steve began.

Lang threw up both hands. "I'll reform. I really will. I'm going to ask that little brunette out and see if she'd like to take me on," he added. "She's dishy, isn't she? I hear she likes to throw things at foreign men. Good thing I'm domestic."

Ahmed looked at Lang with kindling anger, and Steve saw problems ahead. "Better get aboard," Steve told the Arab. "Keep in touch."

Ahmed seemed to realize where he was and to whom he was speaking. He shrugged, as if he'd experienced a minor temporary aberration. "Of course. *Au revoir,* my friend."

He waved and turned to go into the plane, with his entourage at a respectful distance, watching his back.

"Regal, isn't he?" Lang said with reluctant admiration. "I'm sorry to see him go." He grinned at Steve. "Now that this is all over, are you sure you're going to marry that girl of yours? I do like her temper."

"So do I," Steve replied. "Yes, I'm going to marry her. And the next time you point a camera in my general direction, it had better have a lens cap on."

"Yes, sir," Lang said, chuckling. "You'll be glad to know that as of now you are officially unobserved. But if you'd like the results of our straw poll last night, we think you'd give Valentino a run for his money." He threw up a hand and walked away. Wayne followed him a minute later, leaving a sighing Daphne behind with Steve.

"Are you really going to marry Wayne?" Steve asked as they walked back toward the airport entrance.

"The minute we can arrange a ceremony. How about you and Meg?"

"I've got a lot of explaining to do," he replied dryly. "But I think she'll understand. I hope she will, at least."

"She's a sweet woman, Steve. You're very lucky."

"Don't I know it," he mused.

He left Daphne at the office and gave himself the rest of the day off. First on the agenda was to tell Meg the truth.

She was sprawled on the couch going over projection figures the bank had given her when she went to inquire about starting up her own business. Steve came in the old way, through the back door without knocking, and stood over her with relief written all over him.

"It's over," he told her. "Ahmed's on a plane home and the secret agents have gone to root out enemy spies somewhere else. We're free."

She put down her figures and smiled up at him. "So?"

"So," he replied, dropping down beside her, "now that it's over and we're unbugged, I can tell you that Daphne is engaged to that blond agent who hangs out with Lang."

"What?"

"She was the unofficial liaison between us. She had to go where we did."

"But you said ... !"

"I wasn't allowed to tell you what was going on," he told her. "Now that Ahmed's out of danger, there's no more risk."

She frowned. "I thought they were after you."

"Only as a way to get to Ahmed." He got up and poured brandy into a snifter and handed it to her.

"Do I need a drink?" she asked.

"You may."

"Why?"

He smiled down at her. "Ahmed isn't a cabinet minister. He's the sovereign of his country. To put it more succinctly ... he's a king."

Eleven

Meg took a good swallow of the brandy and coughed a little. "That explains a lot," she told him finally. "He did have a more regal bearing than you'd expect in a political flunky. He's out of danger, then?"

"Yes. The overthrow attempt didn't go down. The agency thought he was safer here until it was dealt with. Ahmed's government is friendly to ours and we're fortunate to have access to his strategic location when there are problems in the Middle East. The government is anxious to accommodate him. That's why they supported the company when we decided to sell him our newest jet fighter. It's also why he got top priority protection here when his life was in danger."

"I still can't quite believe it."

"You have to keep his identity to yourself, however," he told her warningly. "Because he'll be back to have another look at his purchase when we've got it closer to completion. His life may depend on secrecy. Even in this country, there are nationals from his kingdom with grudges."

"Poor Ahmed." She frowned. "He must not enjoy being guarded all the time." Another thought came to her. "He's a king, which means that he has to marry a princess or something, doesn't it? He can't just marry for love, can he?"

"I don't know," he said. His silver eyes searched hers. "I'm glad that I got to choose my own wife," he added huskily. "Now that I've waited four years for her, I don't intend waiting any longer."

"You sound very impulsive."

"I'll show you impulsive." He pulled her to her feet and bundled her out the door. Several hours later, the blood tests were complete, the paperwork was underway and the wedding was scheduled for the end of the week.

"You aren't slipping through my fingers again," he chuckled when they walked arm in arm into his own house. "My mother will be delighted. We'll have to phone her tonight. By the way," he added, "I've found three possibilities for your studio. I thought you might like to go and look them over tomorrow."

"I'd love to!" She reached up and hugged him warmly, feeling as if she'd just come home. She closed her eyes with a sigh as they stood together in the deserted house. Steve's housekeeper had long since left a note about cold cuts and gone home. "Am I staying for supper?" Meg murmured.

He turned her to him. "You're staying for good," he said quietly. "Tonight and every night for the rest of your life."

She hesitated. "But, David will expect me..."

He bent and began to kiss her, softly at first, and then with building intensity so that, after a few minutes, she didn't remember her brother's name. But they agreed that one lapse before marriage was enough. And while Meg slept in his arms that night, sleeping was all they did together. They had the rest of their lives for intimacy, he reminded her.

Early the next morning, Steve took Meg around to the studio prospects he'd found for her. She settled on one in a good location with ample parking, not too many blocks from his office.

"Now," she said, smiling as she looked around, "all I have to do is convince the bank that I'm a good credit risk."

He glowered at her. "I've already told you that I'll stake you."

"I know, and I appreciate it," she said, reaching up to kiss him as they stood in the spacious emptiness of the former warehouse. "But this is something I need to do on my own." She hesitated. "Do you understand?"

"Oh, yes," he said with a slow smile. "You sound just like me at your age."

She laughed. "Do I, really?"

He stuck his hands into his pockets and looked around. "You'll need a lot of paint."

"That, and a little equipment, and some employees who'll be willing to work for nothing until I establish a clientele," she added. "Not to mention an advertising budget." She clenched her teeth. Was she biting off more than she could chew?"

"Start with just yourself," he advised. "Less overhead. See if you can time-share with someone who needs a studio at night. Perhaps a karate master. Put up some posters around town in key business windows, such as day-care centers." He grinned at her astonishment. "Didn't I ever tell you that I'm more an idea man than an executive? Who do you think calls the shots on our advertising campaign and trims off fat from work stations?"

"You're amazing!" she exclaimed.

"I'm cheap," he corrected. "I know how to do a lot for a little."

"How about printing?"

"We use a large concern a block away from here. Since they deal in big jobs, they don't cost as much as a small printer would."

She was grinning from ear to ear. She could see it all taking shape. "The only thing is, how will I teach when I can barely walk?" she asked, hesitating.

"Listen, honey, by the time you get your financing, your carpentry done and your advertising out, that ankle will be up to a lot more than you think."

"Truly?"

He smiled at her worried expression. "Really and truly. Now let's get to it. We've got a wedding to go to."

She wondered if she could hold any more happiness. It seemed impossible.

They were married at a small justice of the peace's office, with David and Daphne and Wayne for witnesses. Brianna waited outside with a camera to take pictures.

"I forgot to hire a photographer!" Steve groaned when they exited the office. He was wearing a blue business suit, and a beaming Meg was in a street-length white suit with a hat and veil, carrying a bouquet of lily of the valley.

"That's all right," Brianna told him. "I used to help our dad in the darkroom. He said I was a natural." She said it a little sadly, because she missed her parents, but not in any self-pitying way. "Stand together and smile, now."

They started to, just as a huge black limousine roared up and a tall, dark man leaped from the back seat.

"Am I in time?" Lang asked hurriedly, righting his tie and smoothing back his unruly hair. "I just flew in from Langley, Virginia, for the occasion!"

"Lang!" Meg exclaimed, breaking into a smile.

"The very same, partner," he chuckled. "How about a big kiss?"

Steve stepped closer to his new wife, with a protective arm around her. "Try it," he said.

Lang lifted both eyebrows. "You want me to kiss you, too? *Yeeech!*"

"I do not!" Steve roared.

"That's a fine way to treat a man who flew hundreds of miles to be at your wedding. My gosh, I even brought a present!"

Steve cocked his head and stared at Lang. "A present? What kind of a present?"

"Something you'll both treasure."

He reached into his coat pocket and took out a packet of photographs.

Steve took the photographs and held them as gingerly as if they'd been live snakes. He opened the envelope and peeked in. But the risqué photos he expected weren't there. Instead, they were photos of Meg, from all sorts of camera angles; Meg smiling, Meg laughing, Meg looking reflective.

"Well, what are they?" Meg asked. "Let me see!"

Steve closed up the package and glanced at Lang with a wry smile. "Thanks."

Lang shrugged. "It was the least I could do." He hesitated. "Uh, there's this, too."

He handed Steve a videotape and followed it with a wicked grin. "From the hall camera . . . ?"

Steve eyed him with growing suspicion. "Just how many copies of this did you make?"

"Only one," Lang swore, hand on his heart. "That one. And there are no negatives."

"Lang, you're a good man," Meg told him with conviction.

"Of course I am." He turned to Brianna, still grinning. "Well, hello, hello. How about lunch? I'll take you to this great little seafood joint down the street and buy you a shrimp!"

"A shrimp?" Brianna asked, hesitating.

Lang pulled out the change in his pocket and counted it. "Two shrimps!" he announced.

Brianna smiled, her blue eyes twinkling. "I'd love to," she said. "I really would. But there's someone I have to go and see. Perhaps some other time."

Lang managed to look fatally wounded. "I see. It's because I can only afford two shrimps, isn't it? Suppose," he added, leaning down toward her with a twinkle in his eyes, "I offered to wash plates after and bought you a whole platter of shrimp?" He wiggled his eyebrows.

She laughed. "It wouldn't do any good. But I do appreciate the sentiment." He was very nice, she thought, a little sad under that clownish exterior, too. But she had so many problems, and her stubborn mind would keep winging back to a tall man with a mustache.... It wouldn't be fair to lead Lang on when she had nothing to offer him.

"Ah, well," Lang murmured. "Just my luck to be so handsome and debonair that I intimidate women."

"That's true," Meg told him. "You're just devastating, Lang. But someday, some nice girl will carry you off to her castle and feed you rum cakes and ice cream."

"Sadist," he grumbled. "Go ahead, torment me!"

"We have to go," Steve said. "Thank you all for coming. We both appreciate it."

"Don't mention it," David chuckled, bending to kiss his sister. "Where are you going on your honeymoon?"

"Nowhere," Meg said. "We're going to wall our-
selves up in Steven's house and stay there until the
food all goes moldy in the refrigerator. And after
that," she said smugly, "I've got a business to get underway!"

"Now see what you've done," David groaned. "My
own sister, a career woman!"

"I always say," Steve mused, smiling down at his
wife, "if you can't beat 'em, join 'em."

"That's just what I say," Meg replied. She took her
hand in his, feeling very newly married and adoringly
glancing at the wedding ring on her left hand.

When they got home, Steve lifted her gently in his
arms and started up the staircase to the master bedroom. She was a little nervous, and so was he. But
when he kissed her, the faint embarrassment was gone
forever.

His open mouth probed hers, the intimacy of the
kiss making her weak with desire. He was moving,
walking, and all the time, his mouth was on hers,
gentling her, seducing her.

She didn't come out of the fog of pleasure until he
laid her gently on the bed and undressed her. Then he
started taking off his own clothes. The sight of that
big, hair-roughened body coming slowly into view
froze her in a half-reclining position on the bed. He
was the most incredibly sexy man she'd ever seen.
Their first time, she hadn't been able to look at him
because there had been such urgency. But now there
was all the time in the world, and her eyes fed on him.

He smiled gently as he sat down beside her, his eyes turbulent and full of desire as he leaned over her. "I know," he said softly. "It wasn't like this before. But we have plenty of time to learn about each other now, Meg. A lifetime."

He bent slowly and put his mouth gently to hers. In the long, lazy moments that followed, he taught her how, watching the expressions chase across her shocked face as he made her touch him. He smiled with taut indulgence until she'd completed the task he set for her, and then he held her hands to him and talked to her, coaxed her into relaxing, into accepting the reality of him.

"It isn't so frightening now that you know what to expect, is it?" he asked, his voice deep and tender as he began to gently ease her out of the last flimsy garments that separated skin from skin.

When he had, he raised and looked at her, his body visibly trembling as he studied the rounded, exquisite flush of her perfect body, her silky skin.

His hand went out and tenderly traced her firm breasts, enjoying their immediate response to his touch, her trembling, her audible pleasure.

"You're beautiful, Meg," he whispered when his exploring hand trespassed in a new way. Despite their former intimacy, the touch shocked her. She caught his wrist and gasped. "No, little one," he coaxed, bending to kiss her wide eyes shut. "Don't be embarrassed or afraid of this. It's part of the way we're going to make love to each other. Relax, Meg. Try to put away all those inhibitions, will you? You're my wife. We're married. And believe me, this is perfectly permissible now.''

''I know,'' she whispered back. ''I'll try.''

His mouth brushed over her eyes, her cheeks, down her face to her throat, her collarbone, onto the silken softness of her breasts while he discovered her.

His mouth on her breasts made her shiver. The faint suction he made was as exciting as the way he began to touch her, making little waves of pleasure ripple up her spine. She forgot to be nervous and her body responded to him, lifting to meet his touch. Her eyes opened, because she wanted to see if it was affecting him, too.

It was. His face was taut. His eyes were narrow and glittery as he looked down at her, and she could feel the tension in his powerful body as it curved against hers on the cool sheets.

He nodded. His eyes searched hers and his touch became softer, slower, more thorough. She made a quick, shocked sound, and his hand snaked under her neck to grasp a handful of hair at her nape and arch her face up so that he could see every soft, flushed inch of it.

''You...mustn't...watch!'' she gasped as a hot, red mist wavered her surprised eyes.

''I'm going to,'' he replied. ''Oh, yes, Meg, I'm going to watch you. I'm going to take you right up to the moon. This is going to be our first real night of love. Here and now, Meg. Now, now, now...''

The deep, slow chant was like waves breaking, the same waves that were slamming with pleasure into her body. She held on for dear life and her voice sobbed, caught, as the pleasure grew with each touch, each hot whisper.

He was moving. He was over her, against her. The pleasure was like an avalanche, gaining, gaining, rolling down, pressing down on her, pressing against her, pressing...into...her!

She felt the fierce throb of it, felt the slow invasion, felt the tension suddenly snap into a stinging, white-hot pleasure so unbearably sweet that it made her cry out.

His hands were on her wrists, pinning her, his body above her, demanding, pushing, invading. She heard his harsh breath, his sudden exclamation, the hoarse cry of pleasure that knotted him above her. As he shouted his fulfillment, she fell helplessly from the height to which he'd taken her, fell into a thousand diamond-splintered fragments, each more incredibly hot and sweet than the one before...

He cried out with the pleasure of it, his eyes wide open, his face taut with the strain. "Oh, God...!"

He sank over her, helpless in that last shudder, and she cradled him, one with him, part of him, in a unity that was even greater than the first one they'd ever shared.

She touched his face hesitantly. "Oh, Steven," she whispered, the joy of belonging to him in her eyes, her voice, her face.

He smiled through the most delicious exhaustion he'd ever felt, trying to catch is breath. "Oh, Meg," he replied, laughing softly.

She flushed, burying her face in his throat. "It wasn't...quite like that before."

"You were a virgin before," he whispered, smiling. He rolled over onto his back, bringing her along with him so that she could pillow her cheek on his broad, damp chest. "Are you all right?"

"I'm happy," she replied. "And a little tired."

"I wonder why."

She laughed at the droll tone and burrowed closer. "I love you so much, Steven," she said huskily. "More than my life."

"Do you?" His arms tightened. "I love you, too, my darling." He stroked her hair gently, feeling for the moment as if he had the world in his arms. "I should never have let you go. But I felt something for you so strong that it unnerved me." His arms grew suddenly bruising. "Meg, I couldn't bear to lose you," he said roughly, letting all the secret fears loose. "I couldn't go on living. It was hell without you, those four years. I did wild things trying to fill up the emptiness you left in me, but nothing worked." He drew in a long breath, while she listened with rapt fascination. "I...couldn't let you go again, no matter what I had to do to keep you."

"Oh, Steve, you won't have to!" She kissed him softly, brushed his closed eyes with her lips, clinging fiercely to him as she felt the depth of his love for her and was humbled by it. "I'll never want to go, don't you see? I didn't think you loved me four years ago. I ran because I didn't think I could hold you. I was so young, and I had an irrational fear of intimacy because my sister died having a baby. But I'm not that frightened girl anymore. I'll stay with you, and I'll fight any other woman to the edge of death to keep you!'' she whispered fiercely, clinging to him.

He laughed softly. They were so much alike. ''Yes, I feel the same way.'' He touched her forehead with his lips, relaxing a little as he realized that she felt exactly as he did. ''Ironic, isn't it? We were desperately in love and afraid to believe that something so overwhelming could last. But it did. It has.''

''Yes. I never thought I'd be enough for you,'' she whispered.

''Idiot. No one else would ever be enough.''

She lifted her eyes to his and smiled. ''Are we safe, now?''

''Yes. Oh, yes.''

She flattened her hand over his chest. ''And you won't grind your teeth in the night thinking that I'm plotting ways to run?''

He shook his head. ''You're going to be a responsible businesswoman. How can you run from utility bills and state taxes?''

She smiled at the jibe. ''Good point.''

He closed his eyes, drinking in her nearness, her warm softness. ''I never dreamed of so much happiness.''

''Neither did I. I can hardly believe we're really married.'' Her breath released in a soft sigh. ''I really did love dancing, Steven. But dancing was only a poor second in my life. You came first even then. You always will.''

He felt a surge of love for her that bordered on madness. He rolled her over onto her back and bent to kiss her with aching tenderness.

"I'd die for you," he said unsteadily. His eyes blazed with what he felt, all of it in his eyes, his face. "I hated the world because you wanted to be a ballerina more than you wanted me!"

"I lied," she whispered. "I never wanted anything more than I wanted you."

His eyes closed on a wave of emotion and she reached up, kissing him softly, comfortingly. Tears filled her eyes, because she understood then for the first time his fear of losing her. It humbled her, made her shake all over. She was frightened at the responsibility of being loved like that.

"I won't ever let you down again," she whispered. "Not ever! I won't leave you, not even if you throw me out. This is forever, Steven."

He believed her. He had to. If this wasn't love, it didn't exist. He gave in at last and put aside his fears. "As if I could throw you out, when I finally know what you really feel." He kissed her again, hungrily, and as the fires kindled in her eyes he began to smile wickedly. "Perhaps I'm dreaming again . . ."

She smiled under his hard mouth. "Do you think so? Let's see."

She pulled him down to her. Long, sweet minutes later, he was convinced. Although, as he told her afterward, from his point of view, life was going to be the sweetest kind of dream for the rest of their lives together; a sentiment that Meg wholeheartedly shared.

Meg opened her ballet school, and it became well-known and respected, drawing many young prospective ballerinas. Her ankle healed; not enough to allow her to dance again, but well enough to allow her to teach. She was happy with Steven and fulfilled in her work. She had it all, she marveled.

The performing ballet slippers of flawless pink satin and pink ribbons rested in an acrylic case on the grand piano in the living room. But in due time, they came out again, to be fastened with the slender, trembling hands of Steven and Meg's firstborn, who danced one day with the American Ballet Company in New York—as a prima ballerina.

*   *   *   *   *

SILHOUETTE® _Desire®_

MAN OF THE MONTH: 1993

They're tough, they're sexy...
and they know how to get the
job done....
Caution: They're

MEN AT WORK

Blue collar... white collar... these men are working overtime
to earn your love.

July:	Undercover agent Zeke Daniels in Annette Broadrick's ZEKE
August:	Aircraft executive Steven Ryker in Diana Palmer's NIGHT OF LOVE
September:	Entrepreneur Joshua Cameron in Ann Major's WILD HONEY
October:	Cowboy Jake Tallman in Cait London's THE SEDUCTION OF JAKE TALLMAN
November:	Rancher Tweed Brown in Lass Small's TWEED
December:	Engineer Mac McLachlan in BJ James's ANOTHER TIME, ANOTHER PLACE

Let these men make a direct deposit into your heart.
MEN AT WORK... only from Silhouette Desire!

Take 4 bestselling love stories FREE

Plus get a FREE surprise gift!

Special Limited-time Offer

Mail to Silhouette Reader Service™

3010 Walden Avenue
P.O. Box 1867
Buffalo, N.Y. 14269-1867

YES! Please send me 4 free Silhouette Desire® novels and my free surprise gift. Then send me 6 brand-new novels every month, which I will receive months before they appear in bookstores. Bill me at the low price of $2.24 each plus 25¢ delivery and applicable sales tax, if any.* That's the complete price and—compared to the cover prices of $2.99 each—quite a bargain! I understand that accepting the books and gift places me under no obligation ever to buy any books. I can always return a shipment and cancel at any time. Even if I never buy another book from Silhouette, the 4 free books and the surprise gift are mine to keep forever.

225 BPA AJH6

Name	(PLEASE PRINT)	
Address	Apt. No.	
City	State	Zip

This offer is limited to one order per household and not valid to present Silhouette Desire® subscribers. *Terms and prices are subject to change without notice. Sales tax applicable in N.Y.

UDES-93R   ©1990 Harlequin Enterprises Limited

ANN MAJOR
SOMETHING WILD

Take a walk on the *wild* side with Ann Major's sizzling stories featuring Honey, Midnight...and Innocence!

September 1993 WILD HONEY
Man of the Month
A clash of wills sets the stage for an electrifying romance for J. K. Cameron and Honey Wyatt.

November 1993 WILD MIDNIGHT
Heat Up Your Winter
A bittersweet reunion turns into a once-in-a-lifetime adventure for Lacy Douglas and Johnny Midnight.

February 1994 WILD INNOCENCE
Man of the Month
One man's return sets off a startling chain of events for Innocence Lescuer and Raven Wyatt.

Let your wilder side take over with this exciting series—only from Silhouette Desire!

Silhouette Books has done it again!

Opening night in October has never been as exciting! Come watch as the curtain rises and romance flourishes when the stars of tomorrow make their debuts today!

Revel in Jodi O'Donnell's STILL SWEET ON HIM—
Silhouette Romance #969
...as Callie Farrell's renovation of the family homestead leads her straight into the arms of teenage crush Drew Barnett!

Tingle with Carol Devine's BEAUTY AND THE BEASTMASTER—
Silhouette Desire #816
...as legal eagle Amanda Tarkington is carried off by wrestler Bram Masterson!

Thrill to Elyn Day's A BED OF ROSES—
Silhouette Special Edition #846
...as Dana Whitaker's body and soul are healed by sexy physical therapist Michael Gordon!

Believe when Kylie Brant's McLAIN'S LAW—
Silhouette Intimate Moments #528
...takes you into detective Connor McLain's life as he falls for psychic—and suspect—Michele Easton!

Catch the classics of tomorrow—*premiering* today—
only from ❤ *Silhouette*

Don't miss these additional titles by favorite author
DIANA PALMER!

Silhouette Desire®

#05643	THE BEST IS YET TO COME	$2.75	☐
#05715	THE CASE OF THE CONFIRMED BACHELOR +	$2.89	☐
#05733	THE CASE OF THE MISSING SECRETARY +	$2.89	☐
	+ Most Wanted Series		

Silhouette Romance.™

#08819	EVAN*	$2.59	☐
#08843	DONAVAN*	$2.59	☐
#08910	EMMETT*	$2.69	☐
	*Long, Tall Texans		

Silhouette® Books

#48242	DIANA PALMER COLLECTION	$4.59	☐
	(2-in-1 collection)		
#48254	TO MOTHER WITH LOVE '93	$4.99	☐
	(short-story collection also featuring Debbie Macomber and Judith Duncan)		
#48267	HEATHER'S SONG	$4.50	☐
#48268	FIRE AND ICE	$4.50	☐

TOTAL AMOUNT	$	
POSTAGE & HANDLING	$	
($1.00 for one book, 50¢ for each additional)		
APPLICABLE TAXES**	$	_____
TOTAL PAYABLE	$	_____
(check or money order—please do not send cash)		

To order, complete this form and send it, along with a check or money order for the total above,
payable to Silhouette Books, to: *In the U.S.:* 3010 Walden Avenue, P.O. Box 9077, Buffalo,
NY 14269-9077; *In Canada:* P.O. Box 636, Fort Erie, Ontario, L2A 5X3.

Name: _____

Address: _____ City: _____

State/Prov.: _____ Zip/Postal Code: _____

**New York residents remit applicable sales taxes.
Canadian residents remit applicable GST and provincial taxes.   DPBACK1

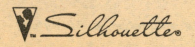